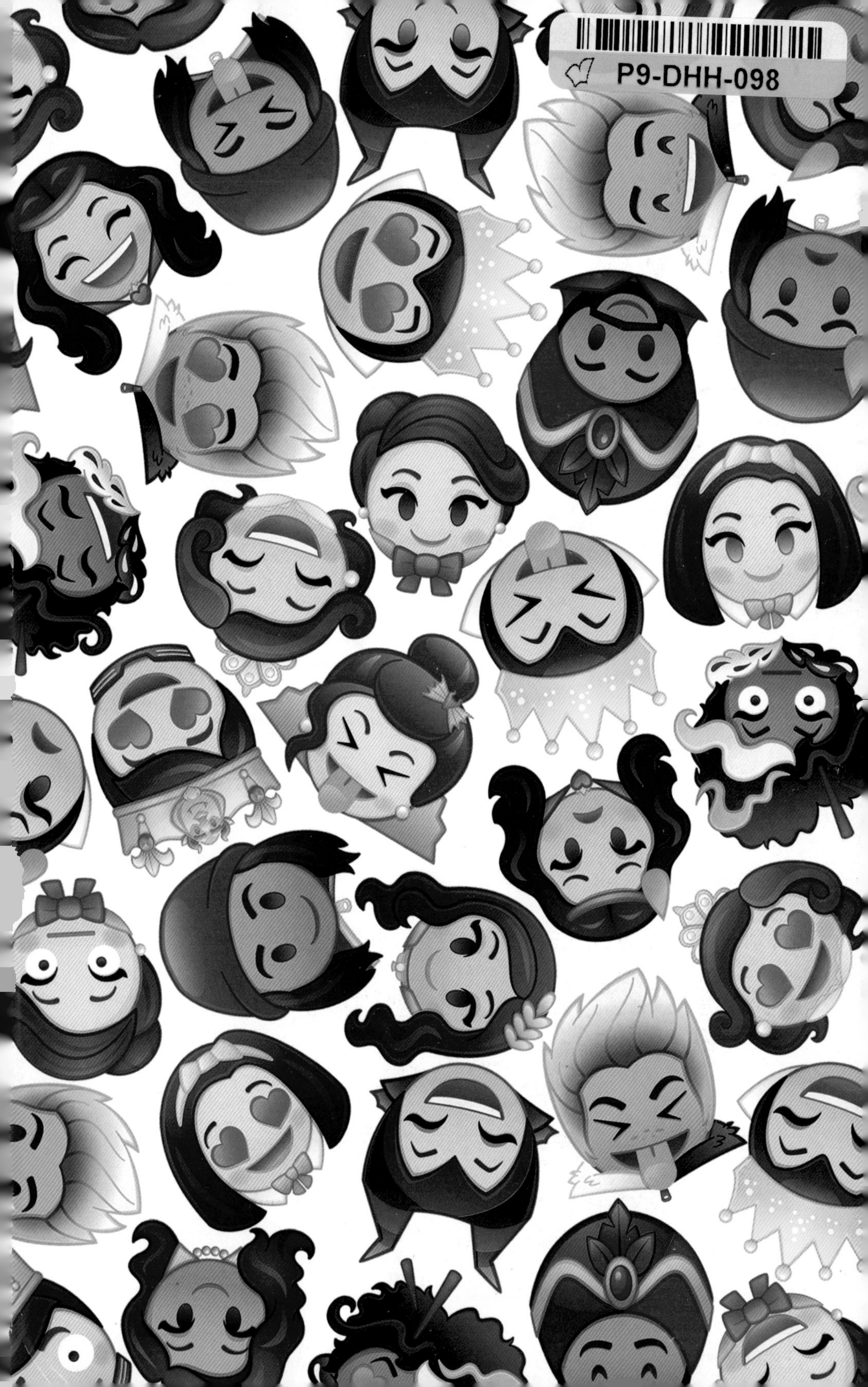

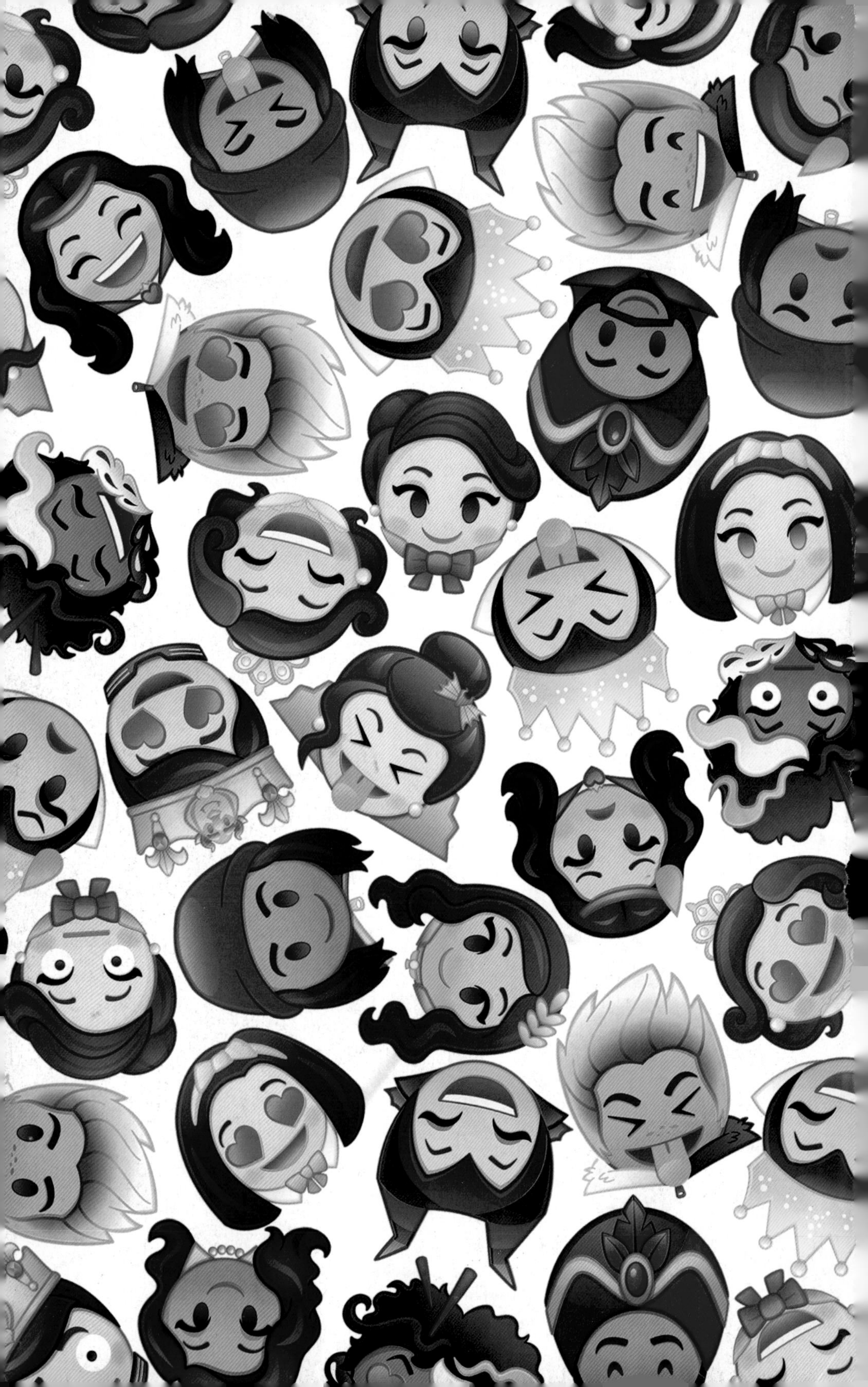

Disney Descendants

As Told By Disney emoji

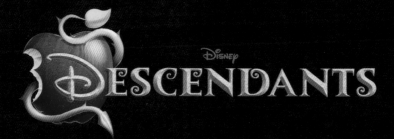

Published simultaneously in the United States and Canada by Joe Books Ltd, 489 College Street, Suite 203, Toronto, ON M6G 1A5.

www.joebooks.com

First Joe Books edition: April 2018

Print ISBN: 978-1-77275-734-7

Library and Archives Canada Cataloguing in Publication information is available upon request.

Printed and bound in Canada

1 3 5 7 9 10 8 6 4 2

Disney DESCENDANTS

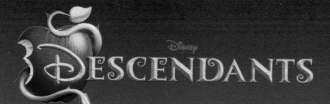

As Told By Disney emoji

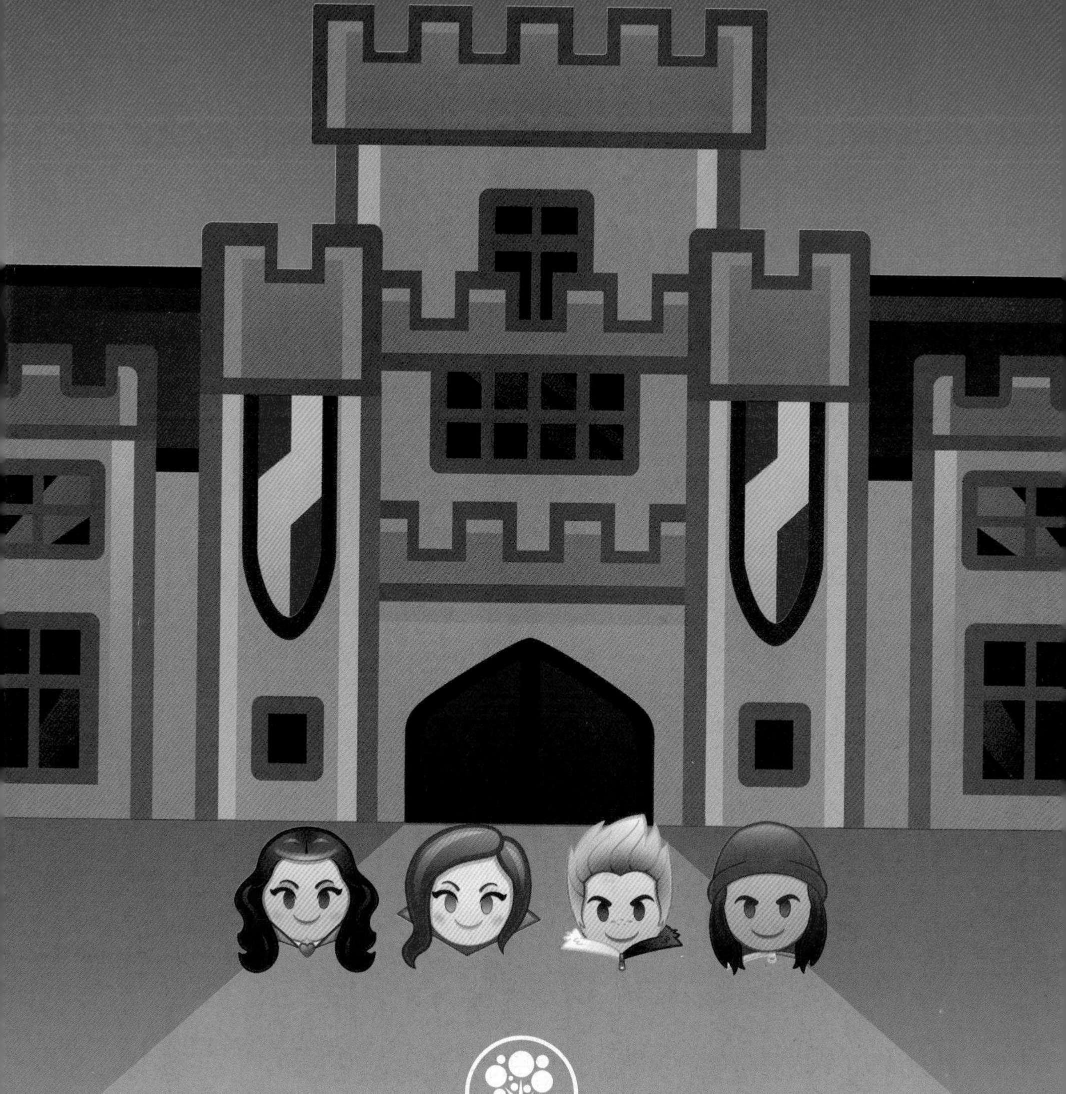

JOE BOOKS

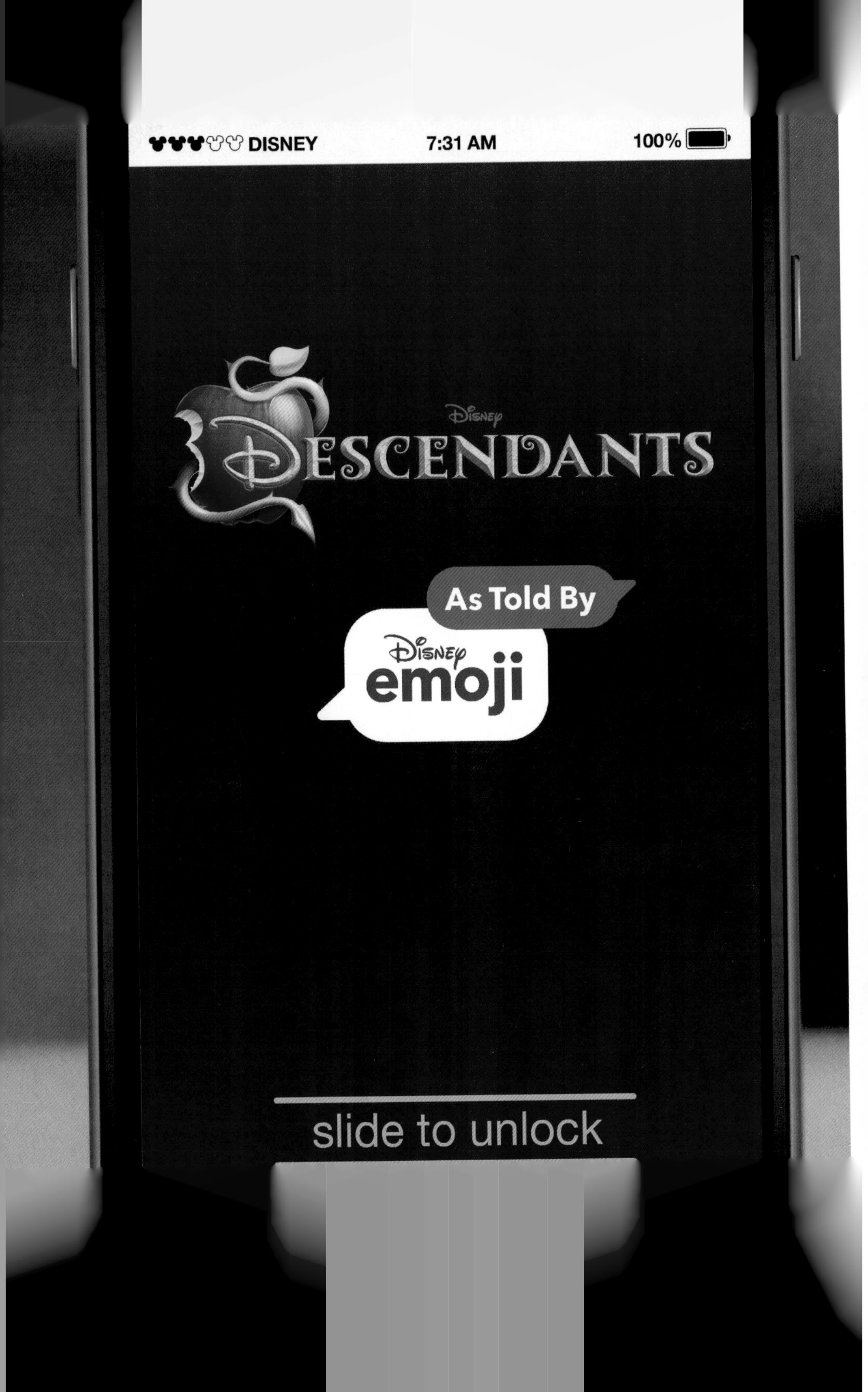
DISNEY
7:31 AM
100%
Disney
DESCENDANTS
As Told By
Disney
emoji
slide to unlock

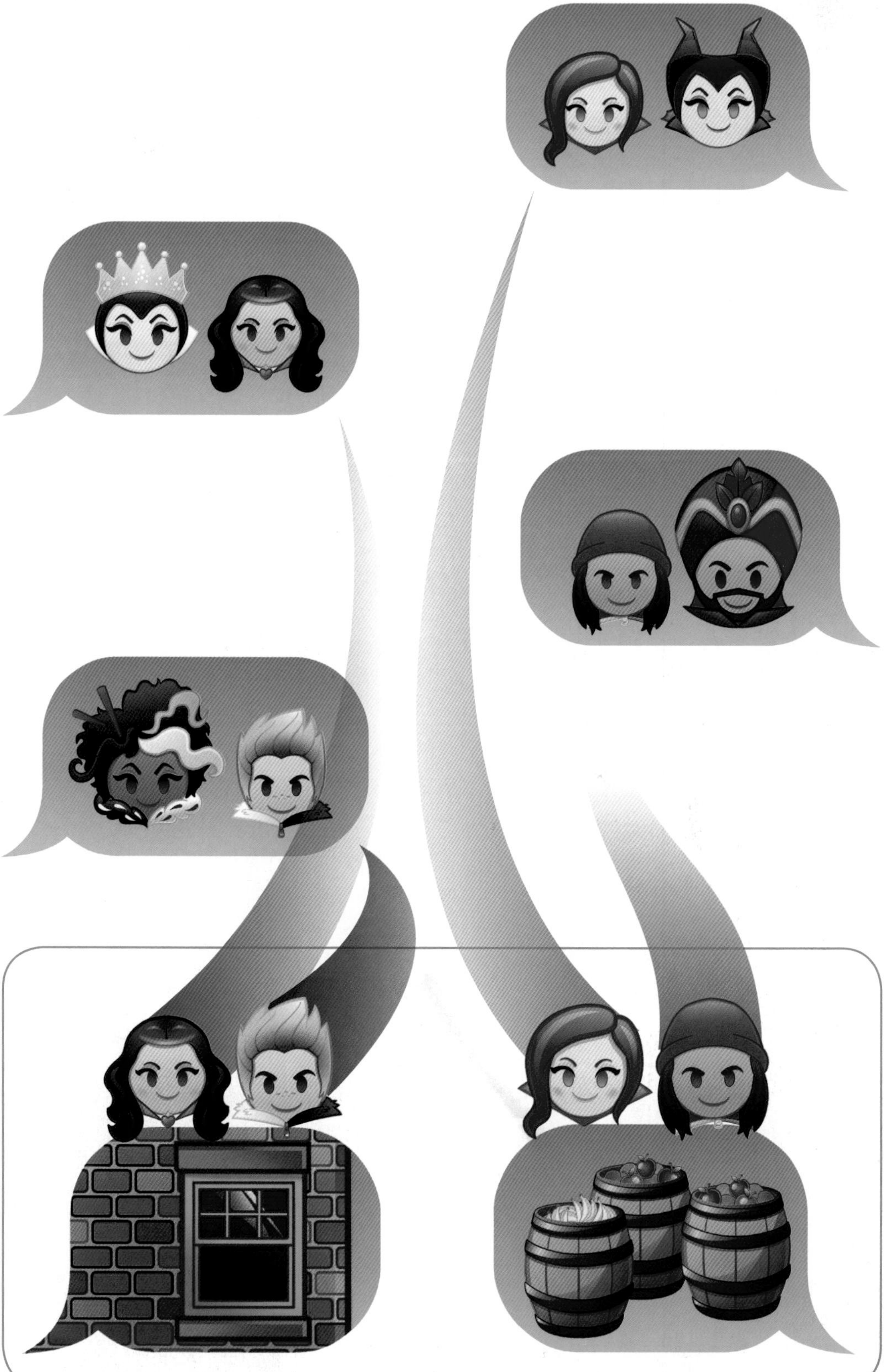

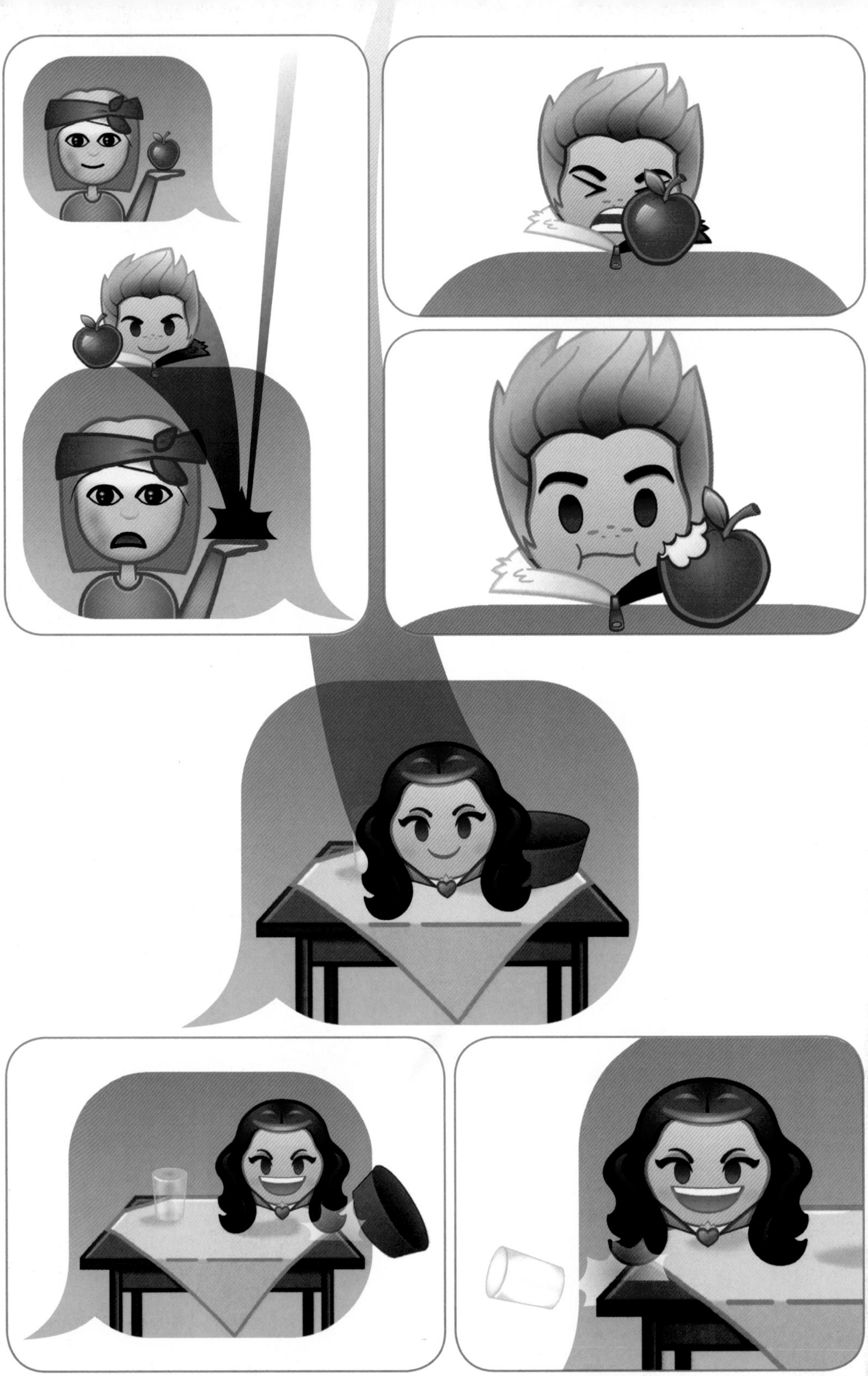

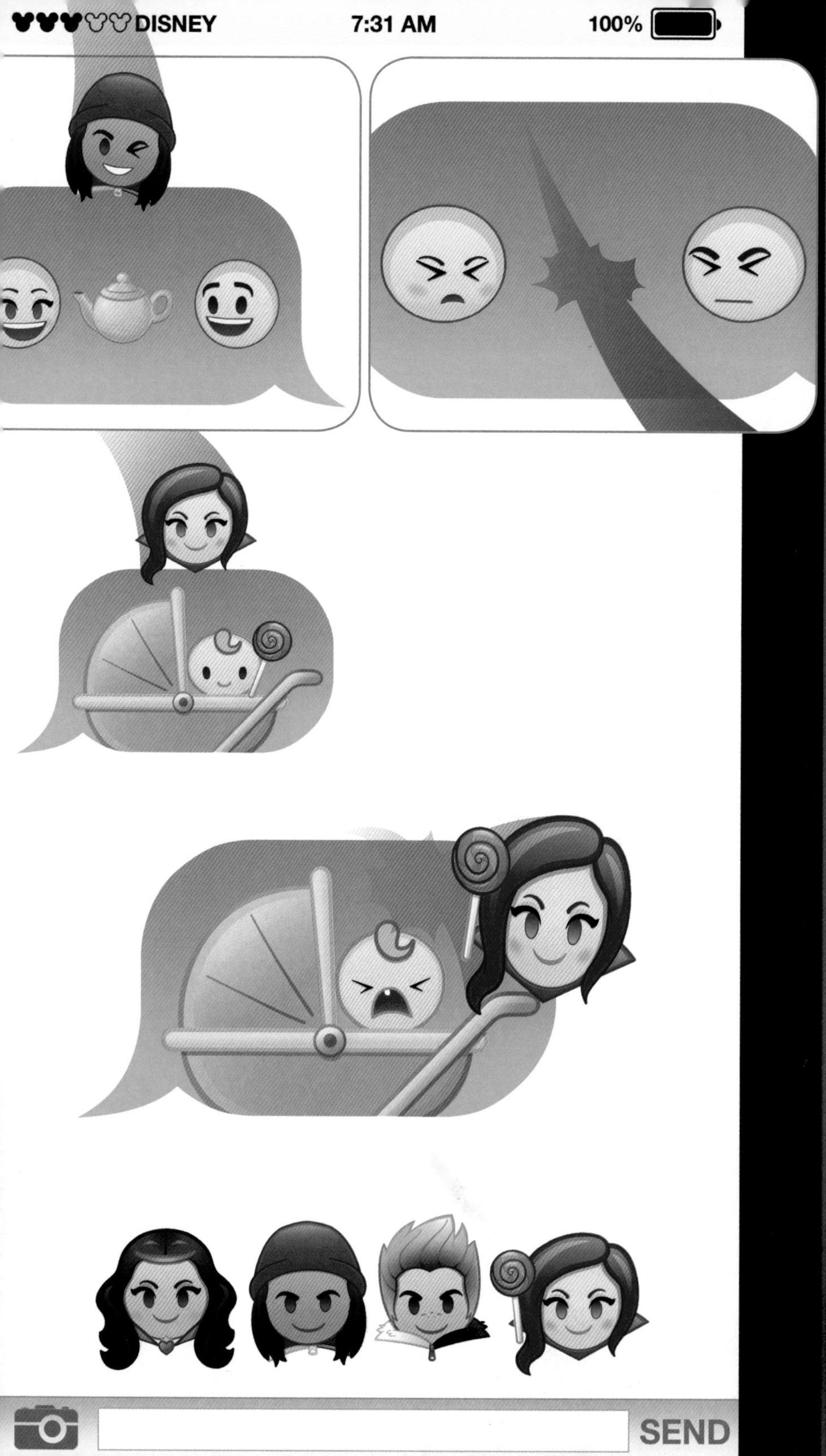
DISNEY
7:31 AM
100%
SEND

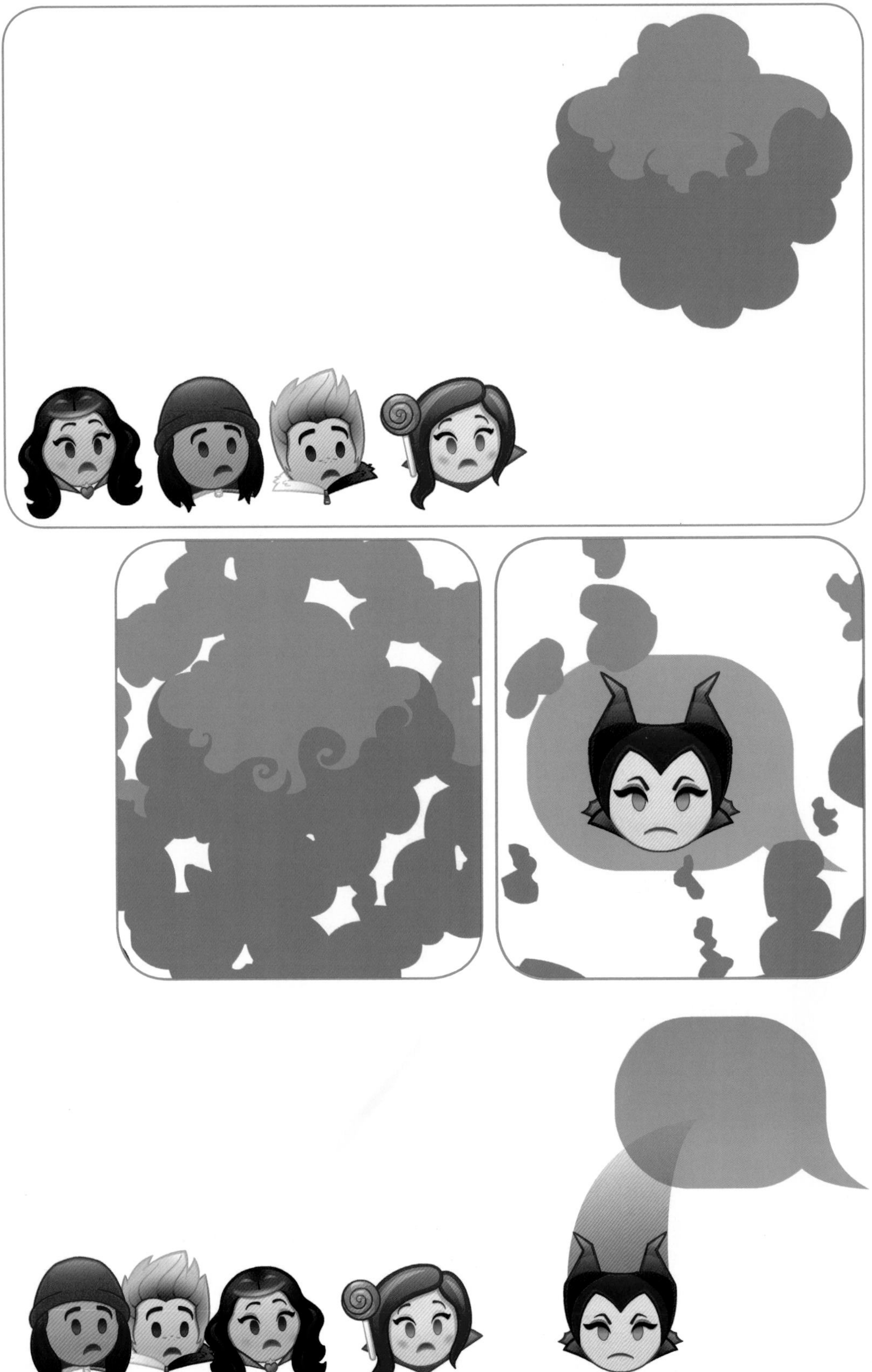

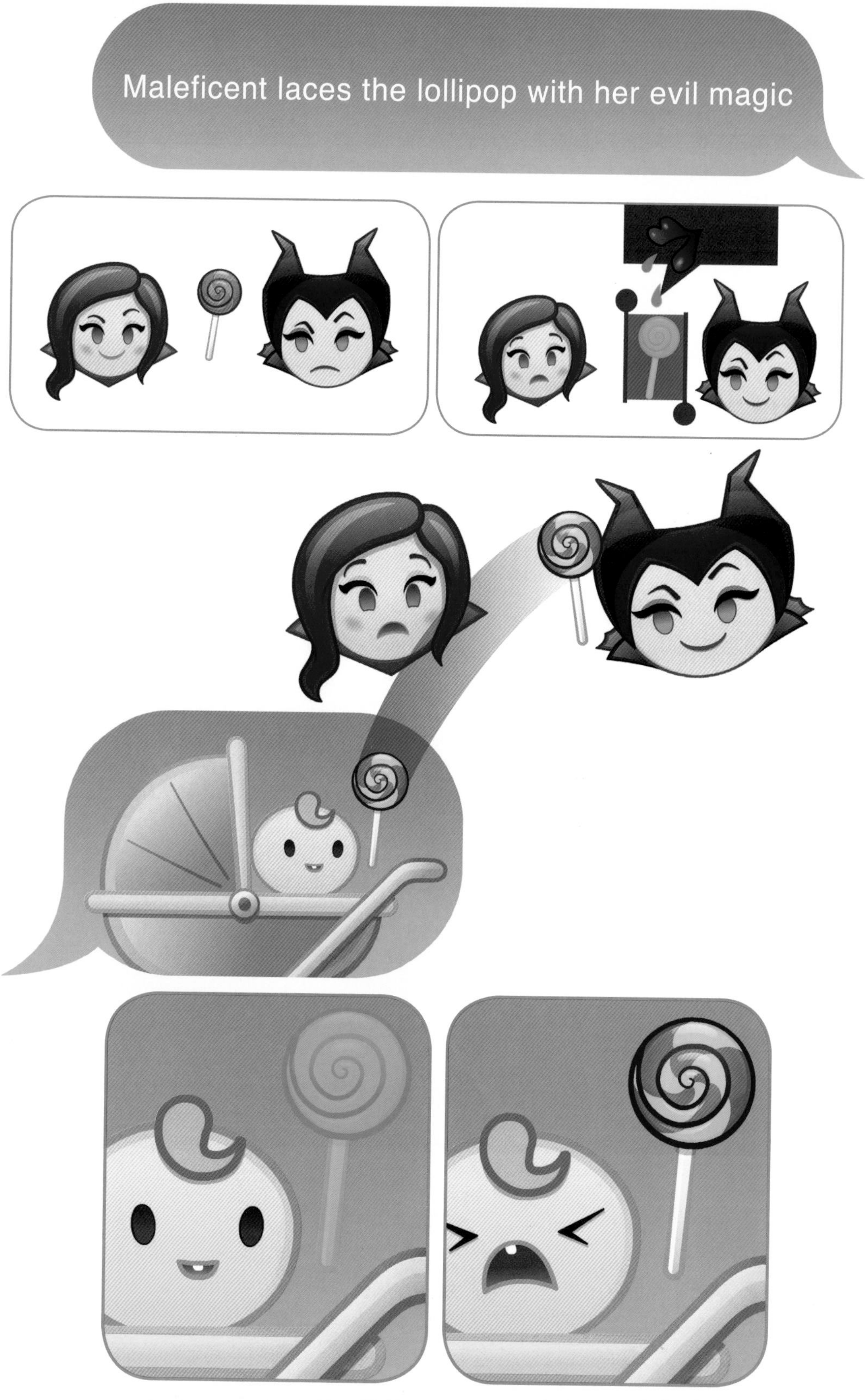
Maleficent laces the lollipop with her evil magic

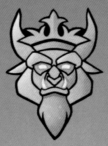

YOU ARE INVITED TO AURADON!

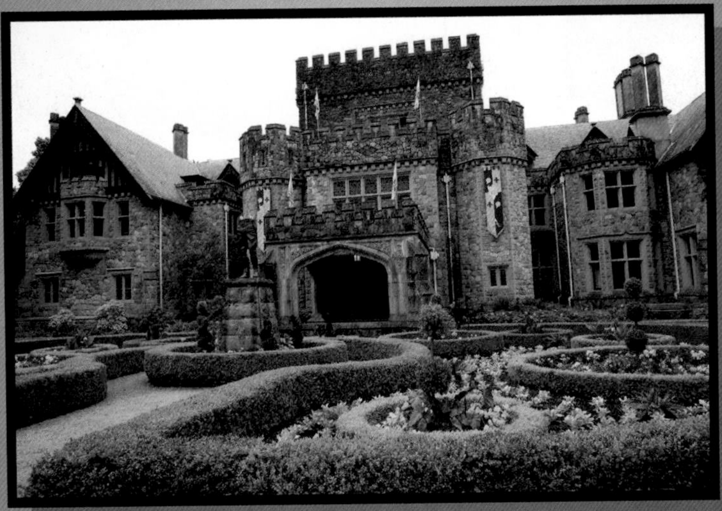

FROM:

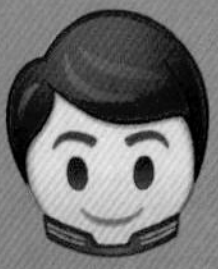

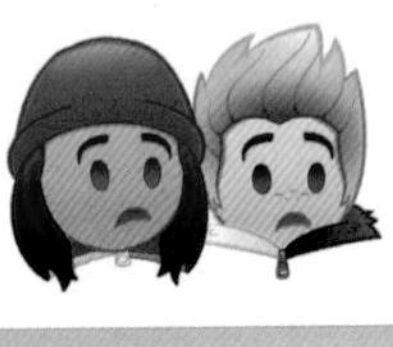

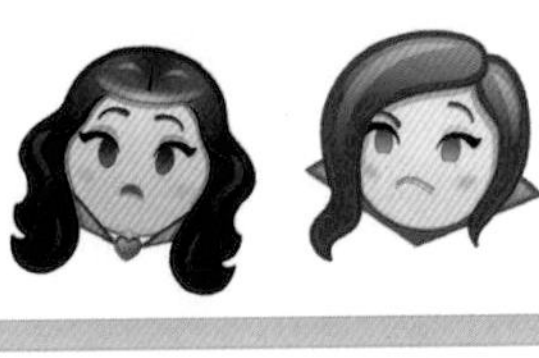

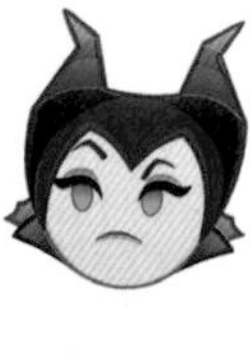

SEND

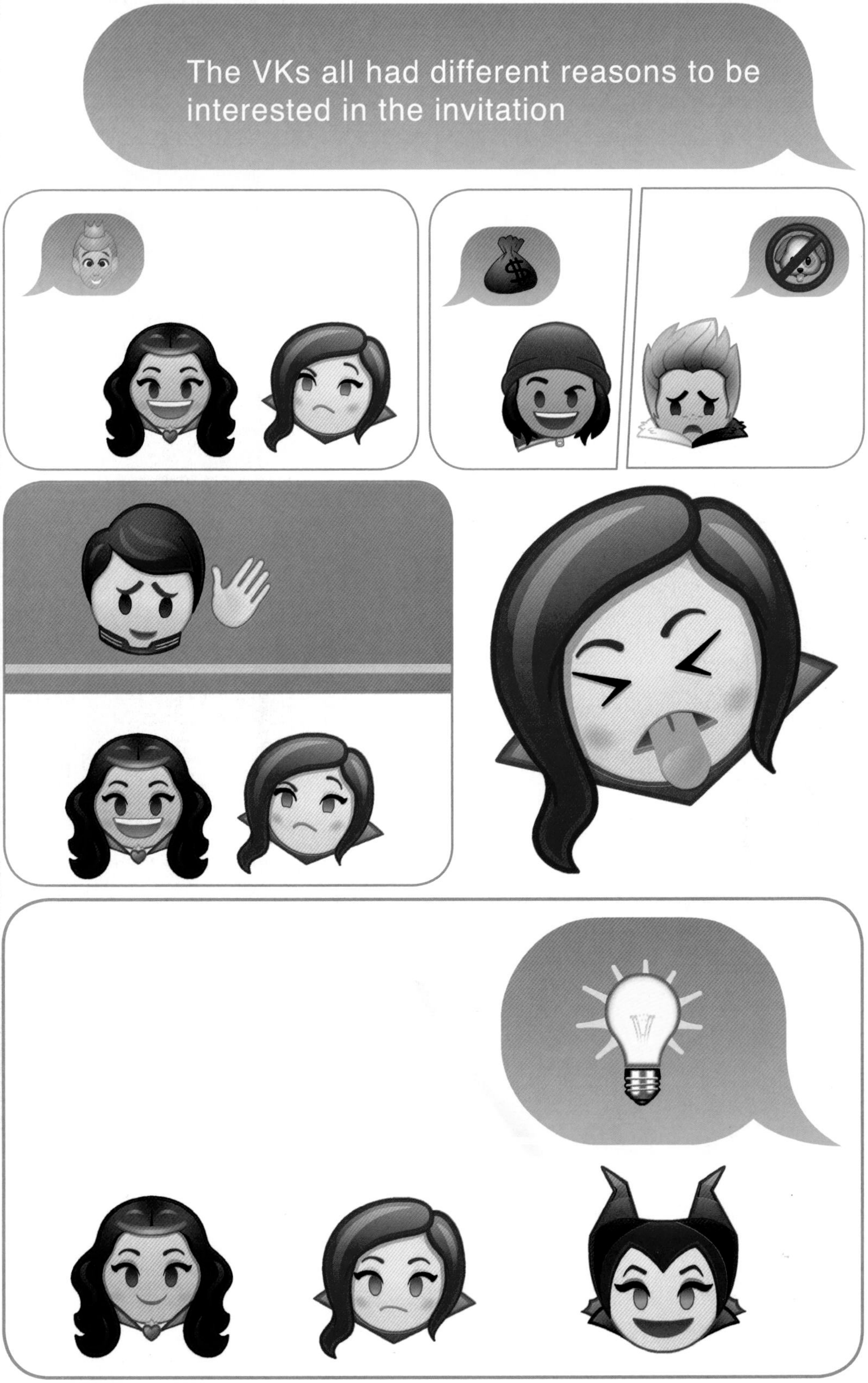
The VKs all had different reasons to be interested in the invitation

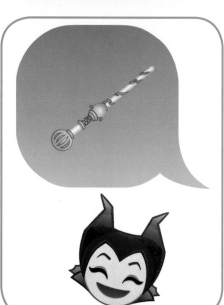

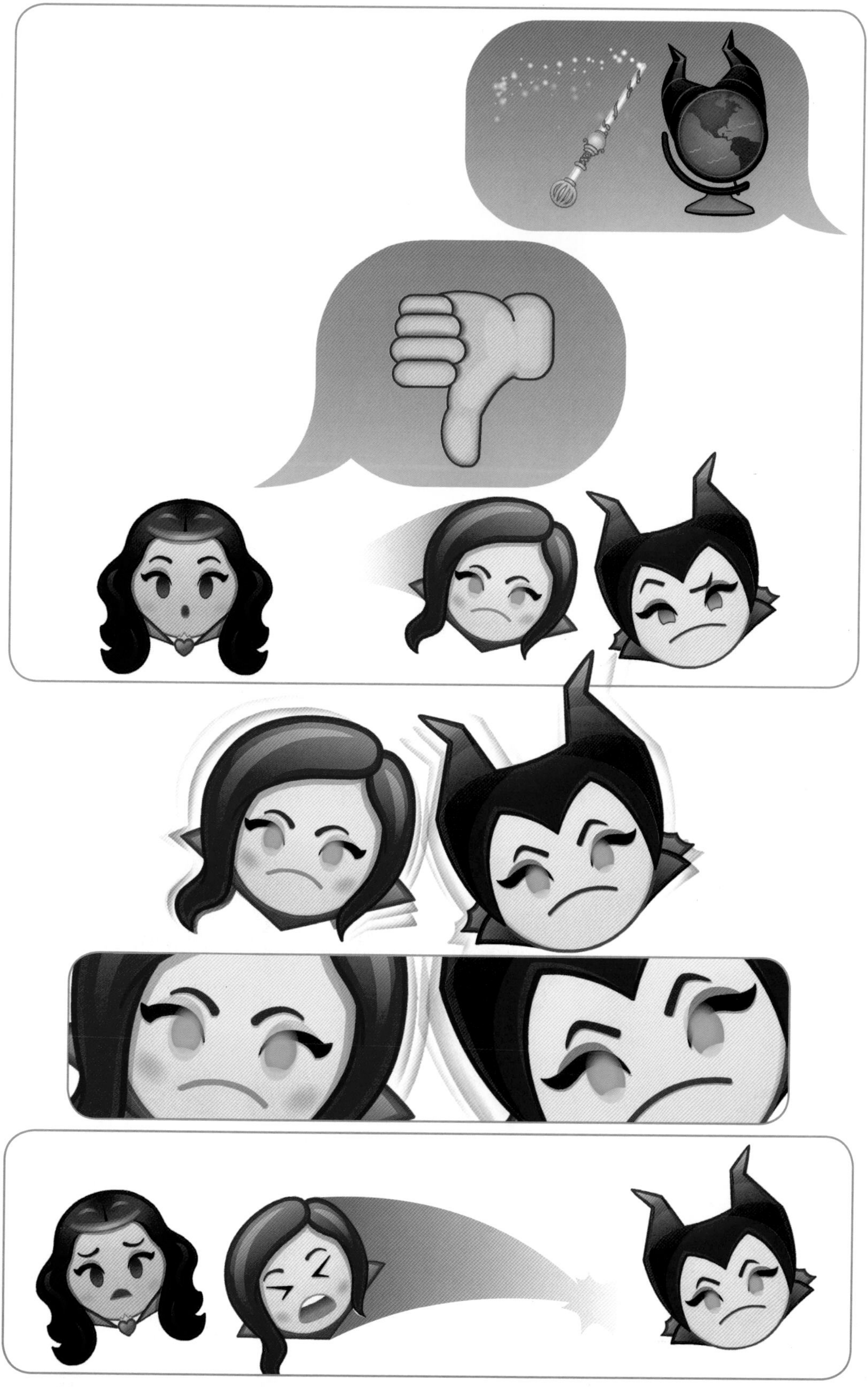

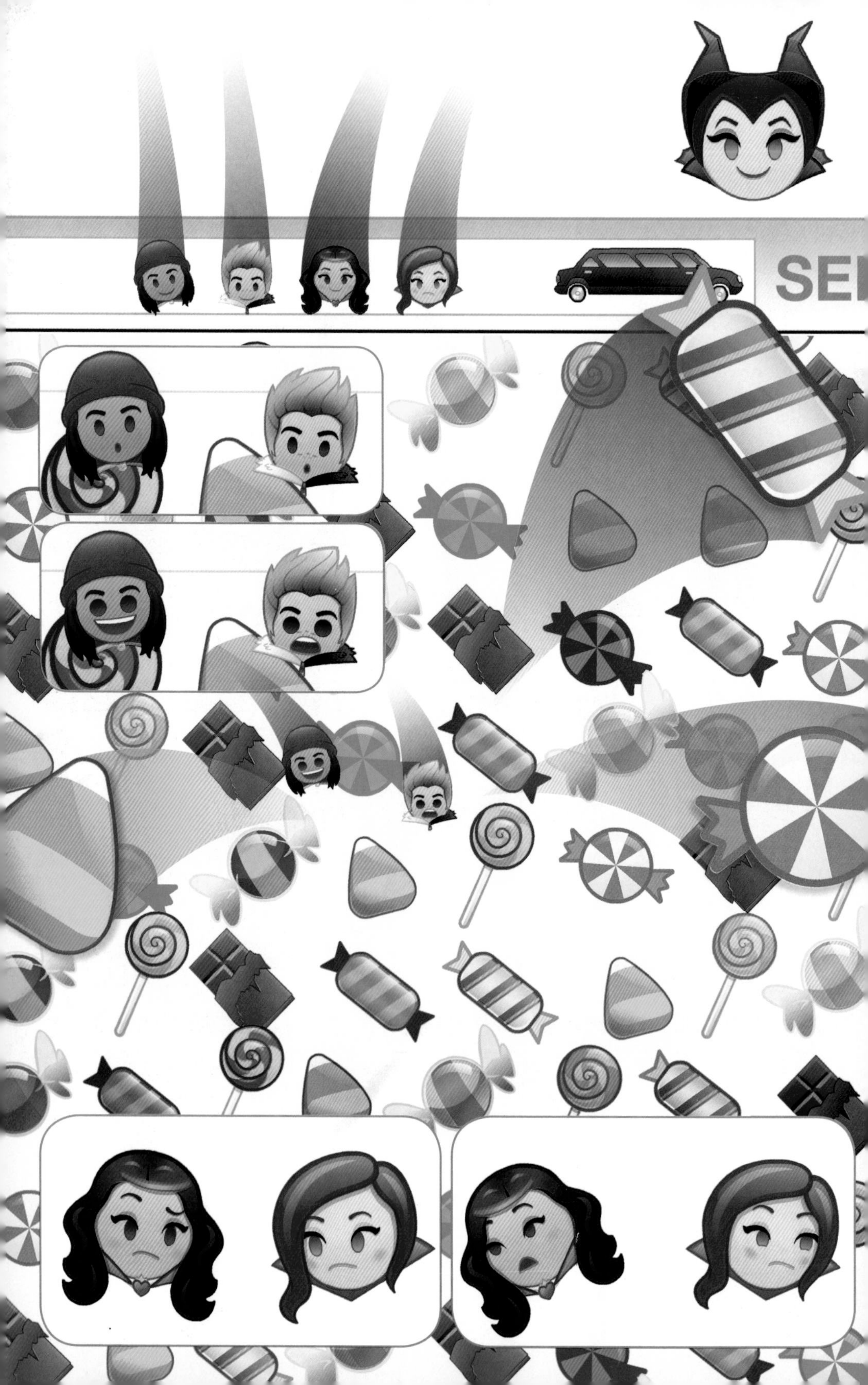

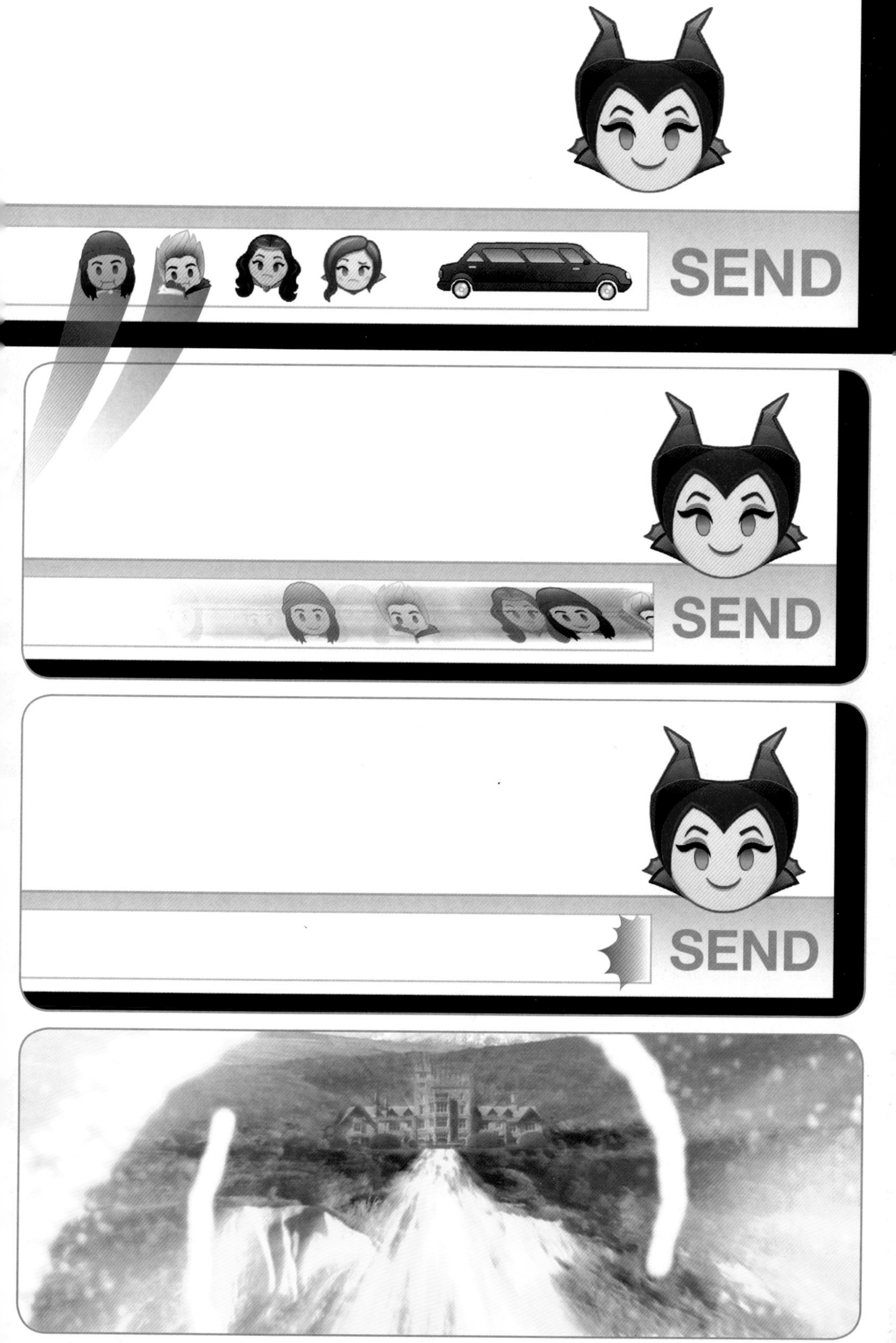
SEND
SEND
SEND

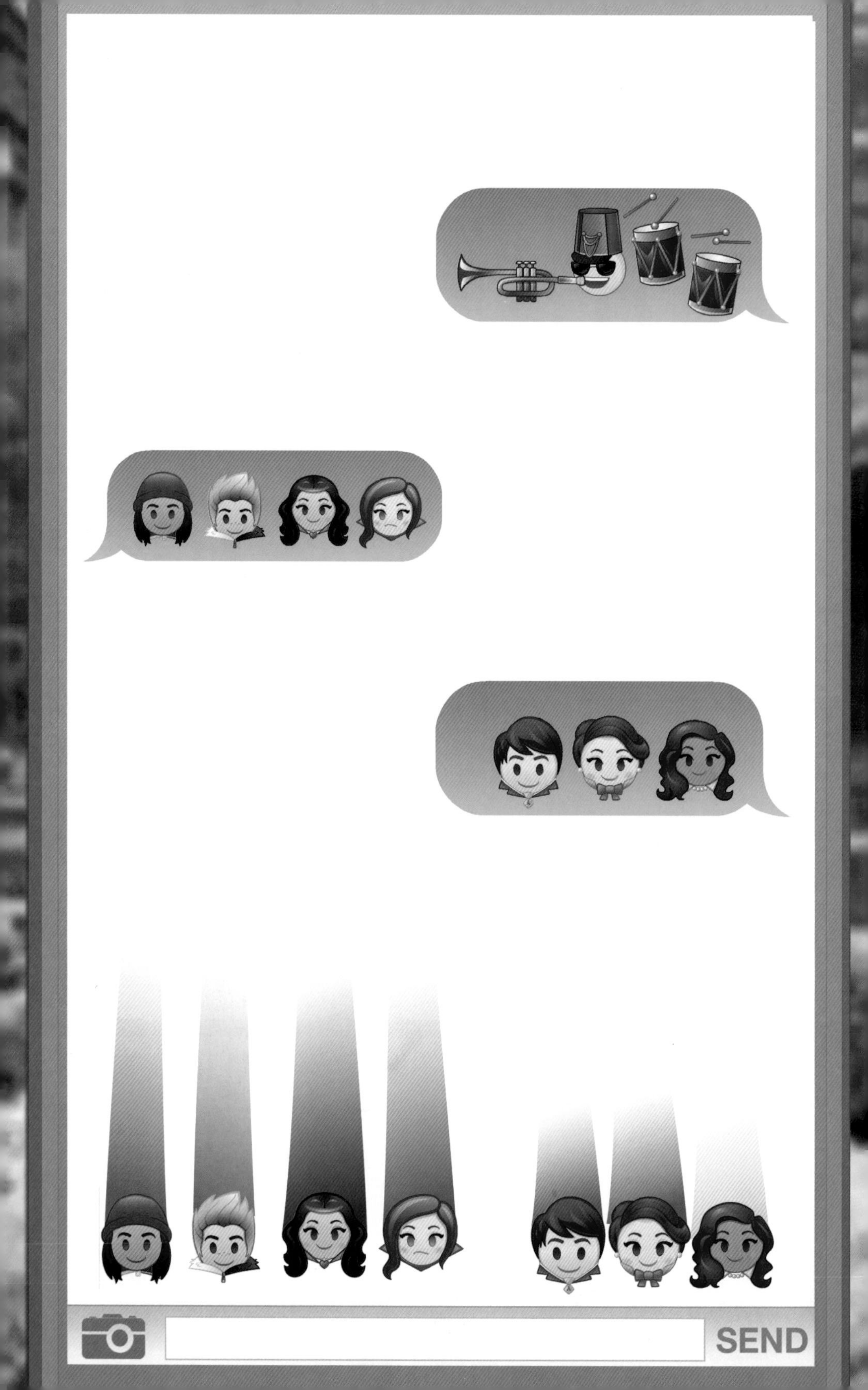
SEND

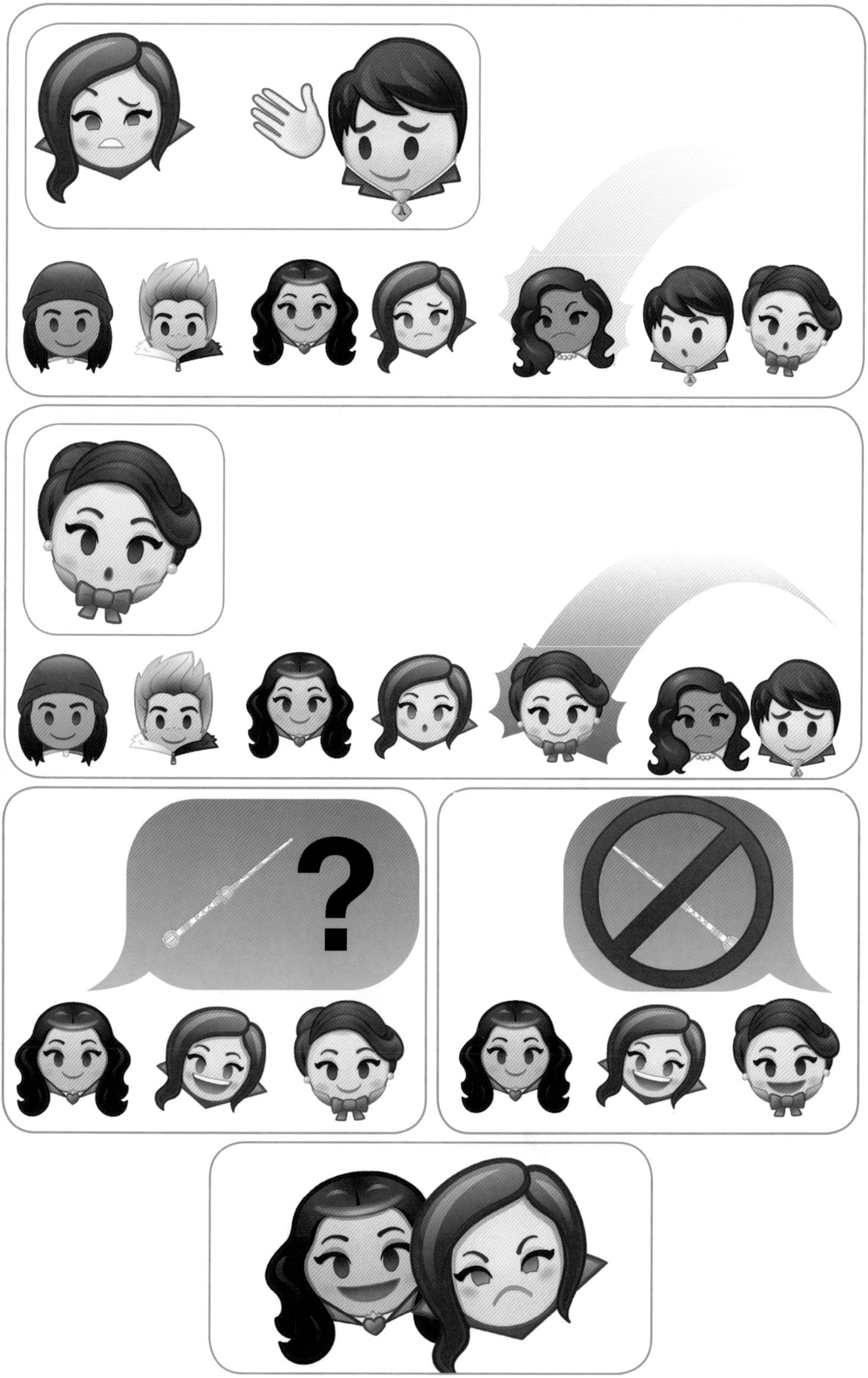
?

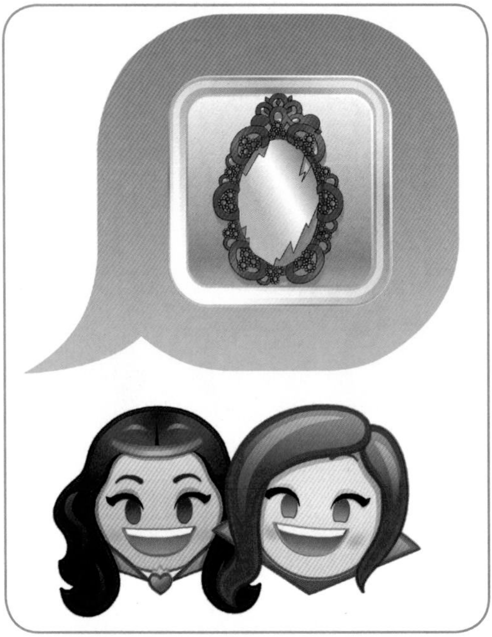

Mal uses Evie’s magic mirror to locate the wand

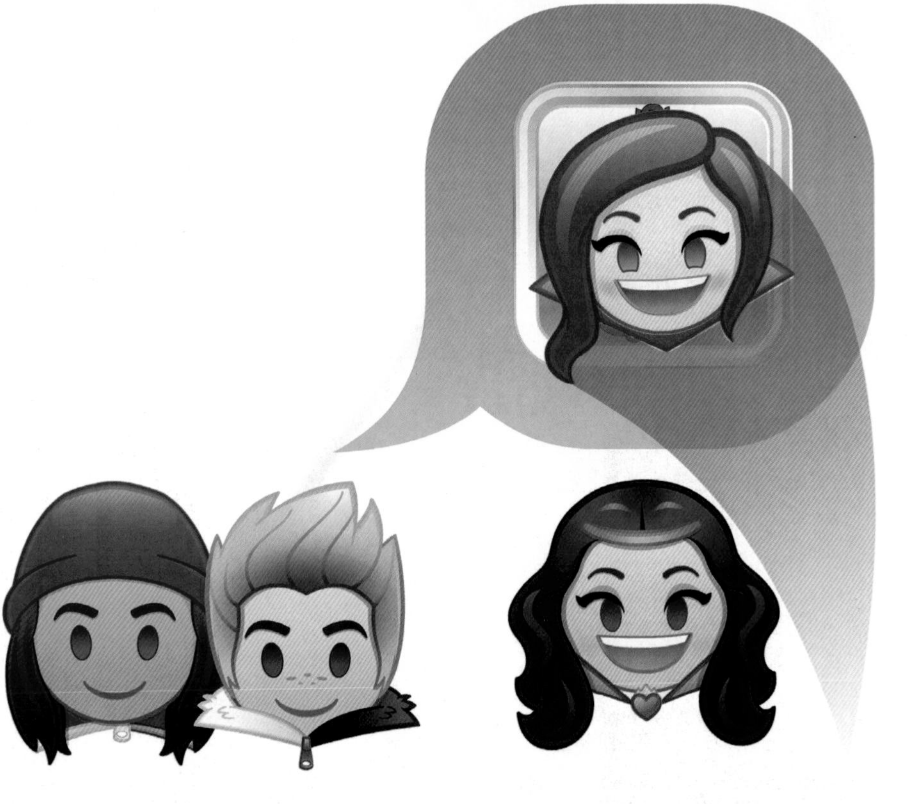

Find:

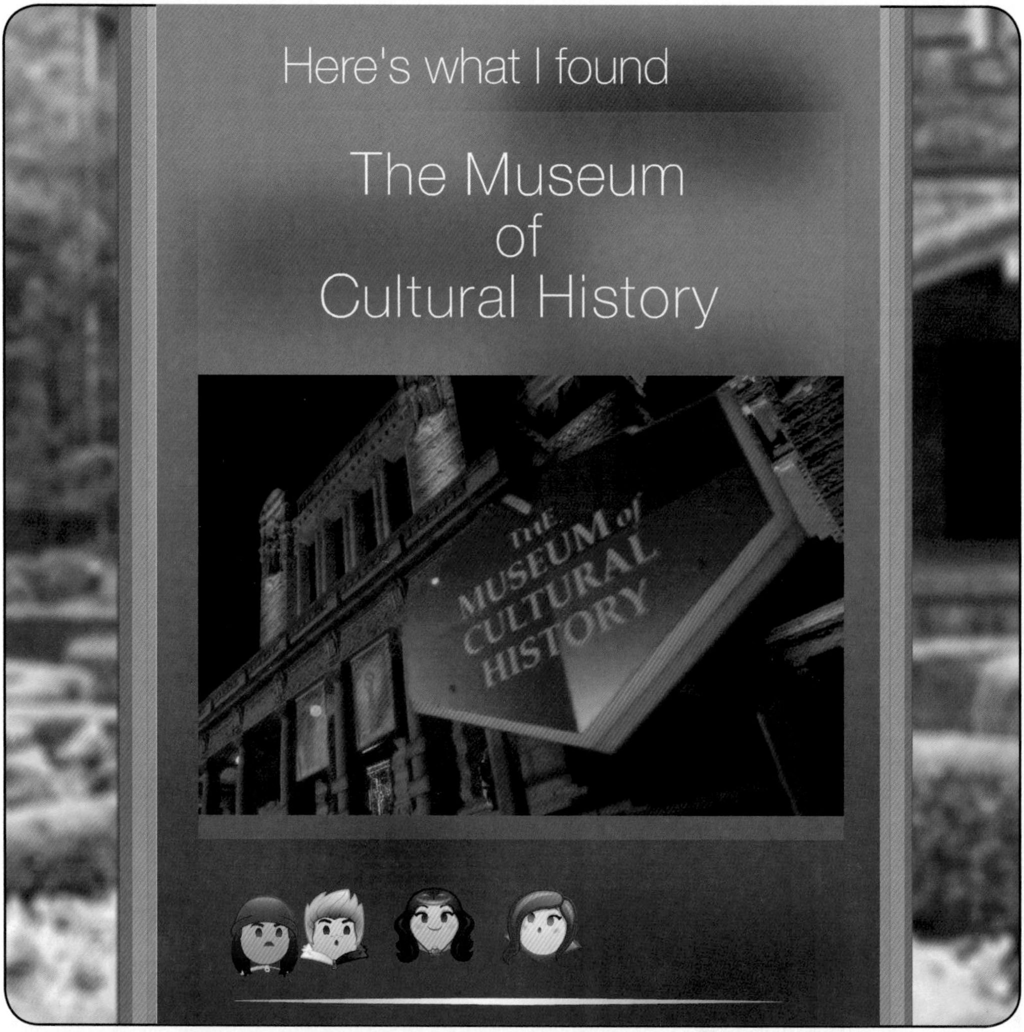
Here's what I found
The Museum of Cultural History
THE MUSEUM of CULTURAL HISTORY

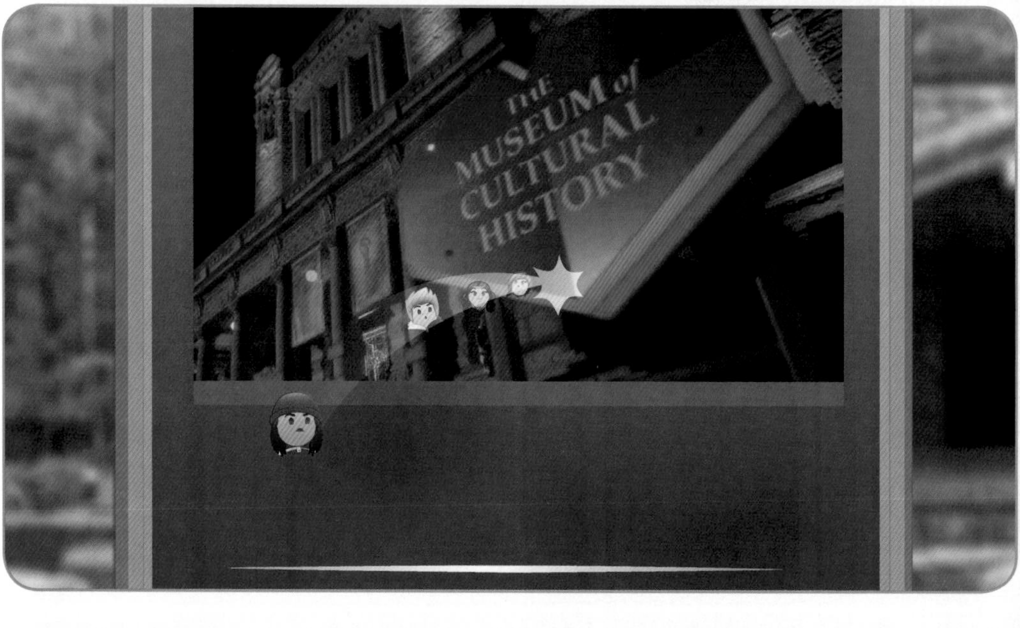
THE MUSEUM of CULTURAL HISTORY

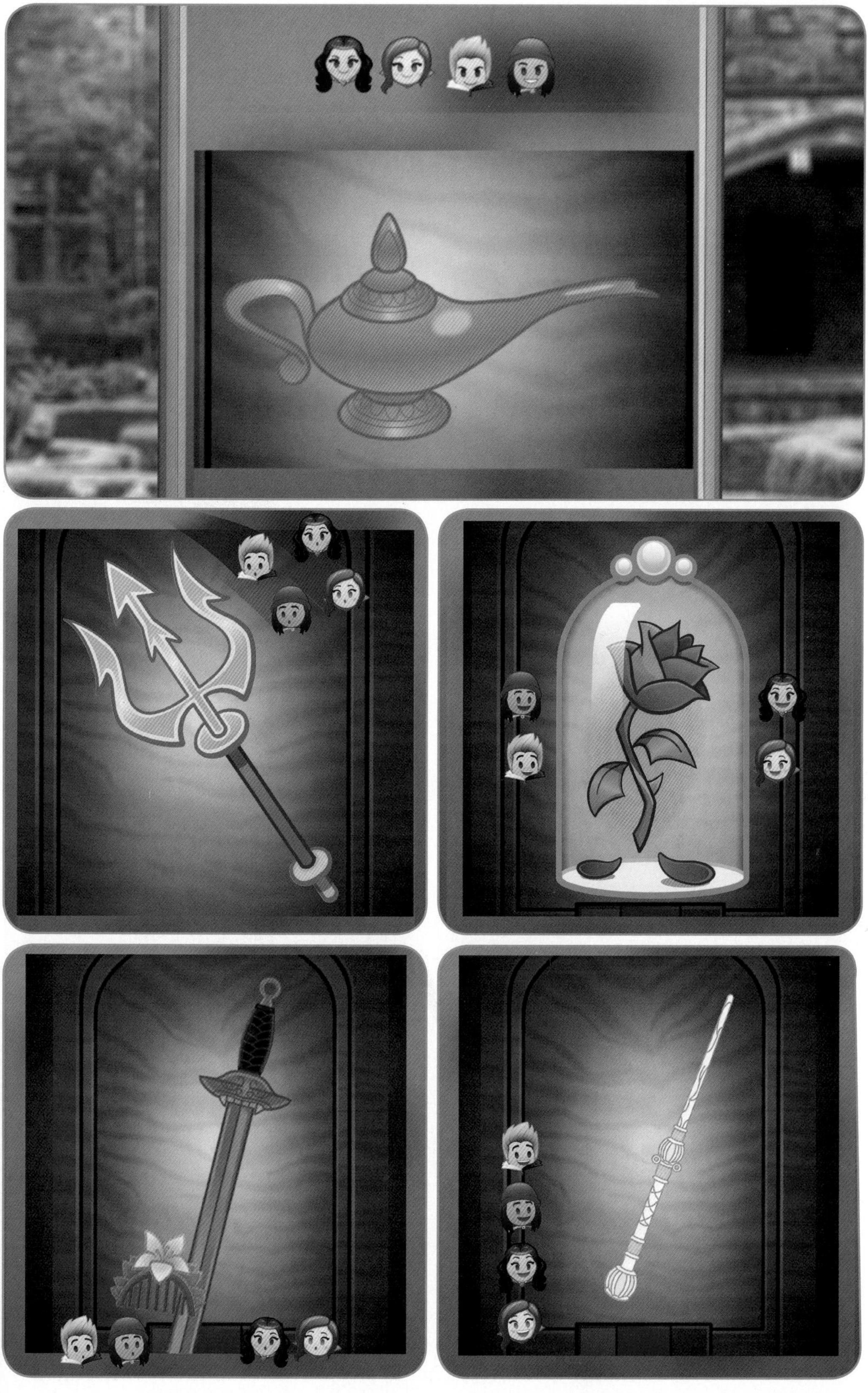

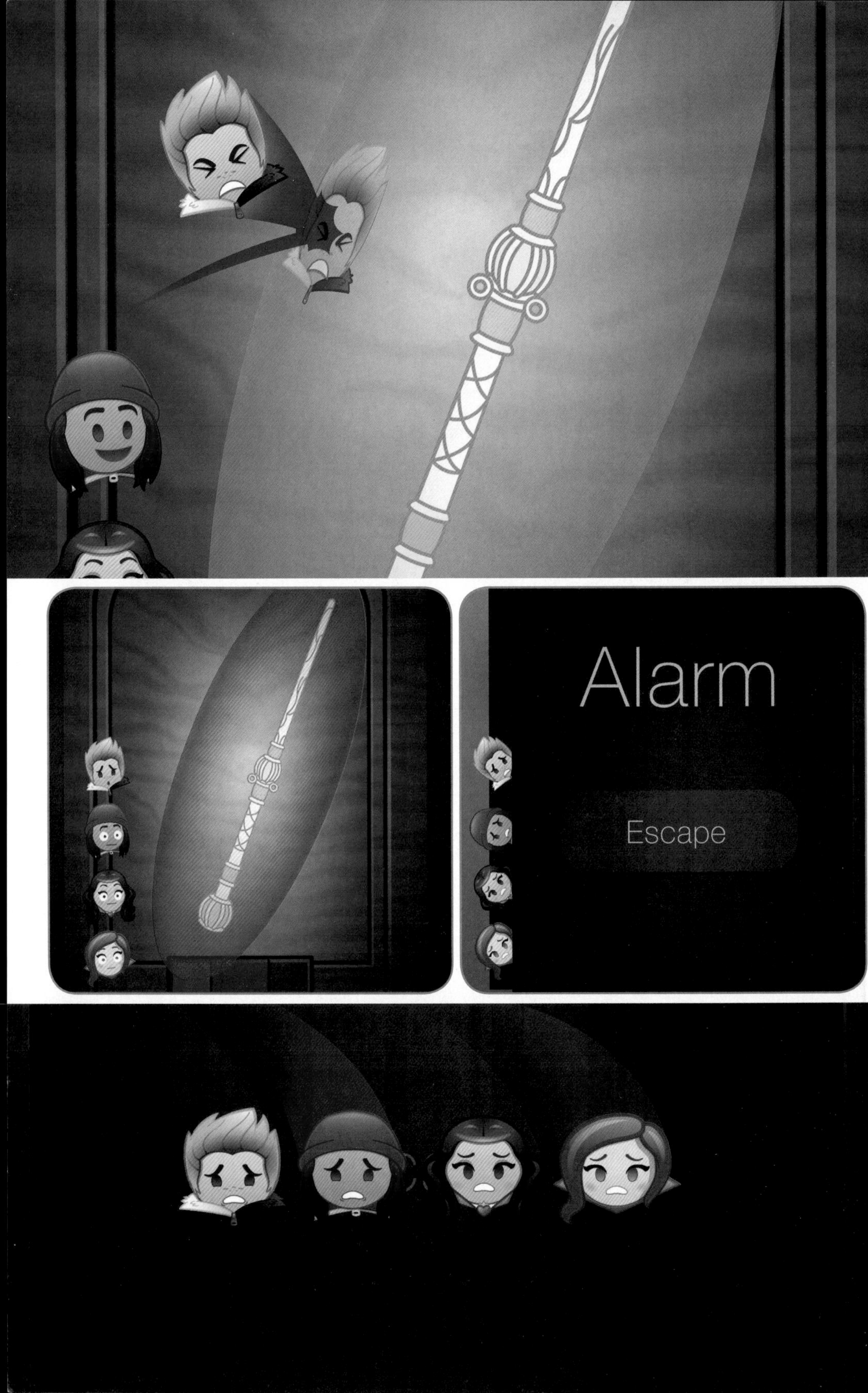
Alarm
Escape

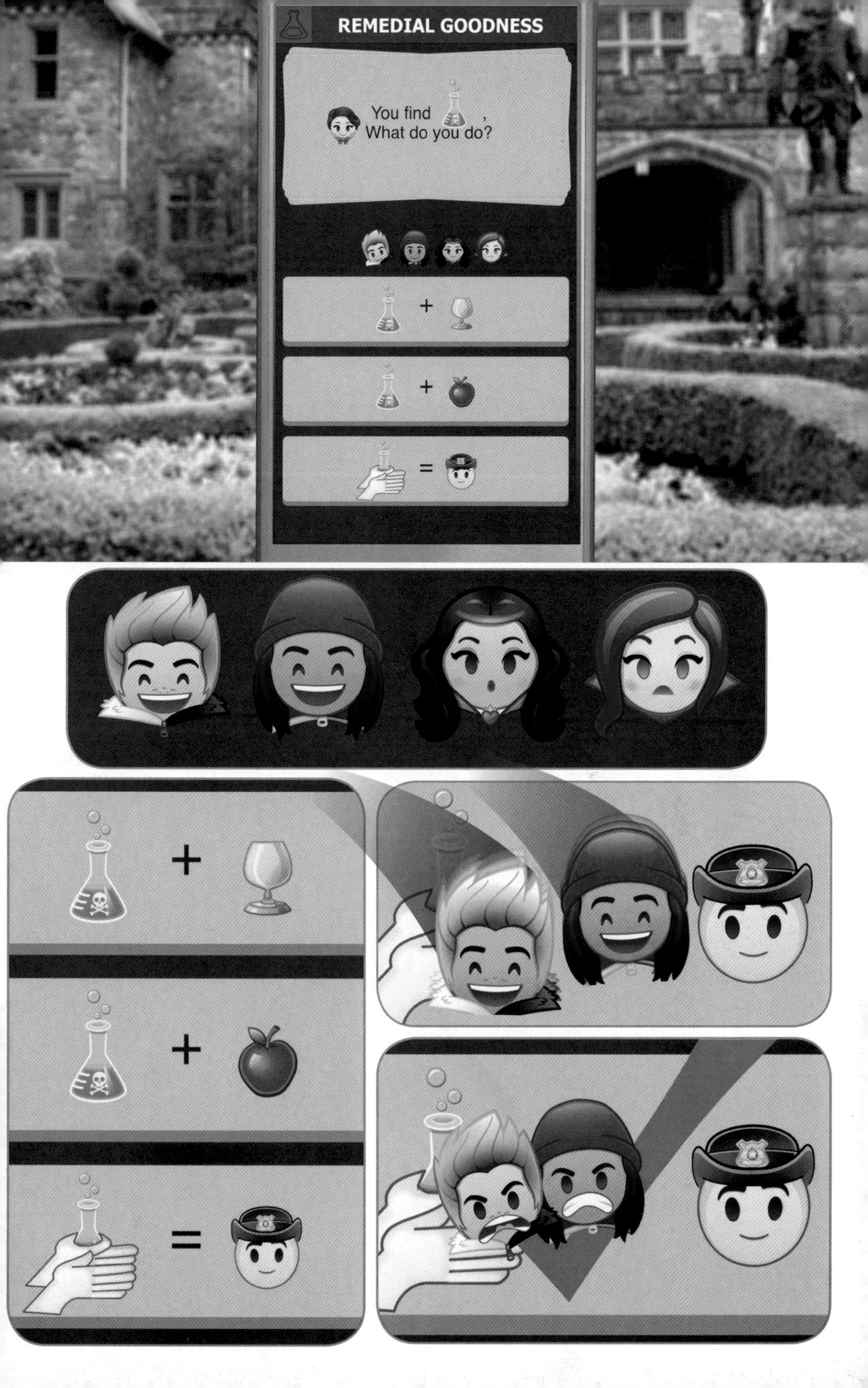
REMEDIAL GOODNESS
You find , What do you do?
+
+
=

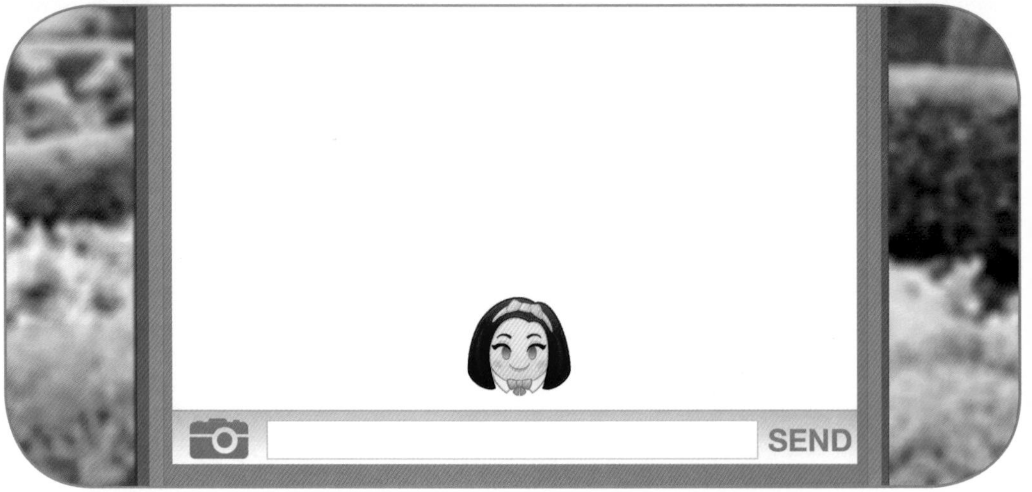
SEND
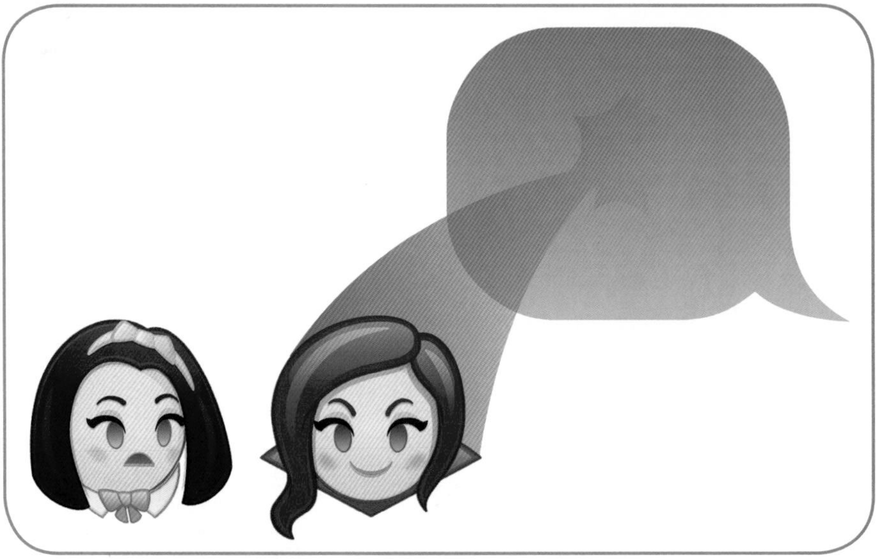
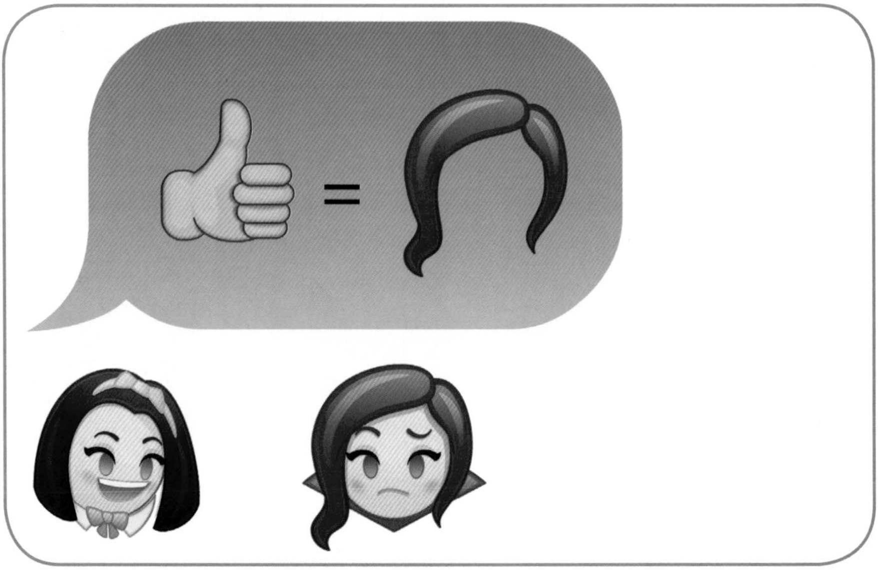

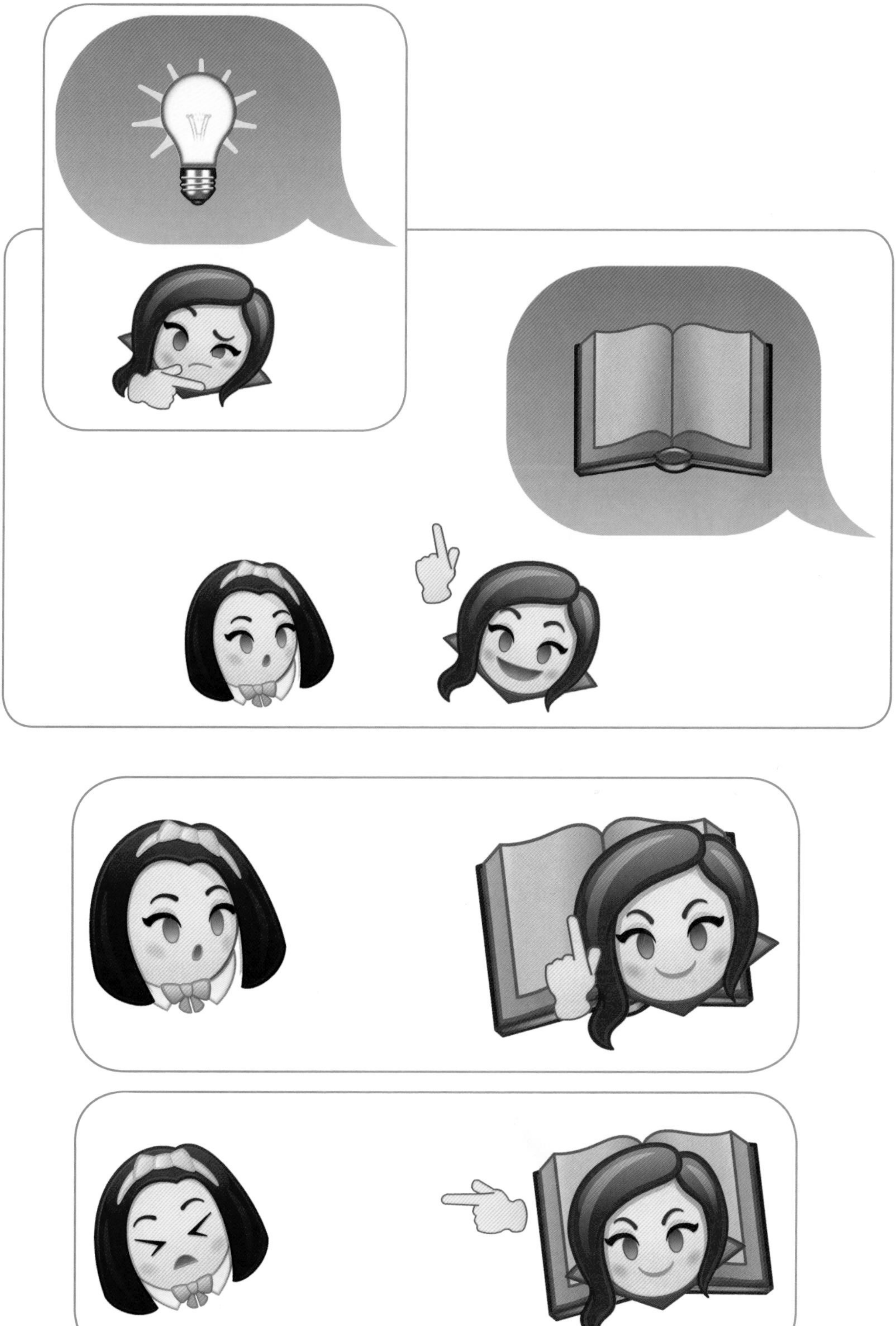

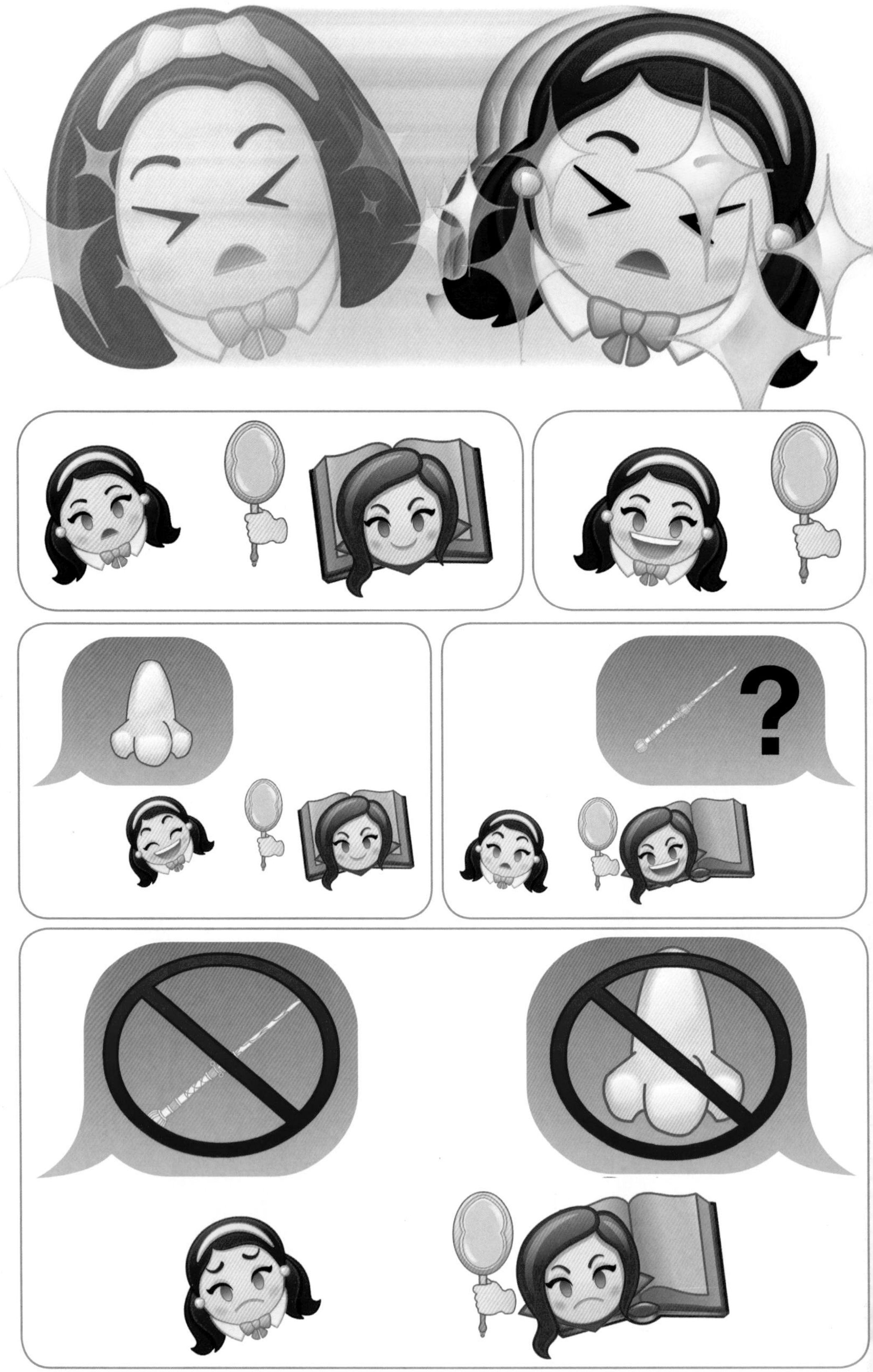
?

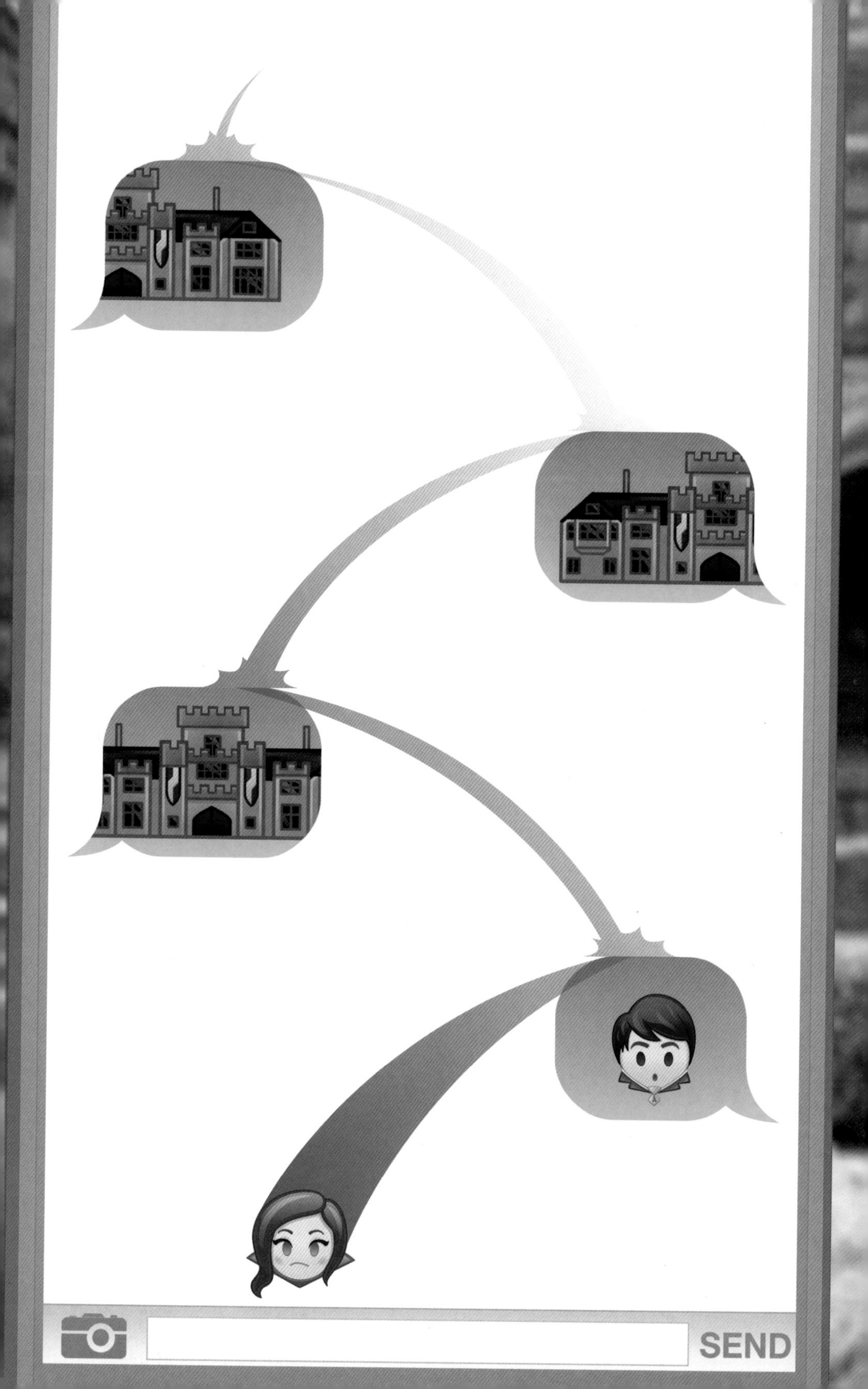
SEND

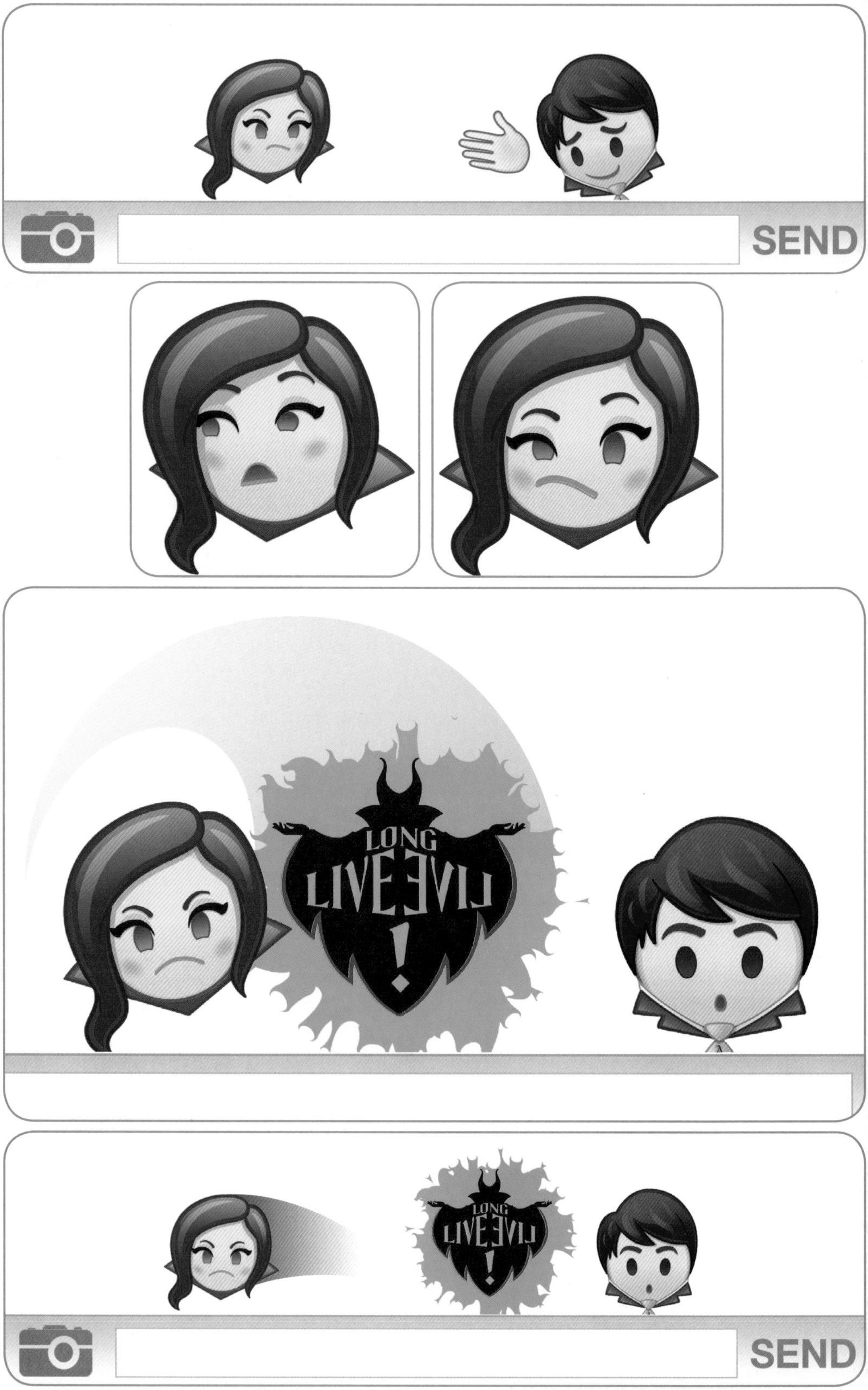
SEND
LONG
LIVE EVIL
!
LONG
LIVE EVIL
!
SEND

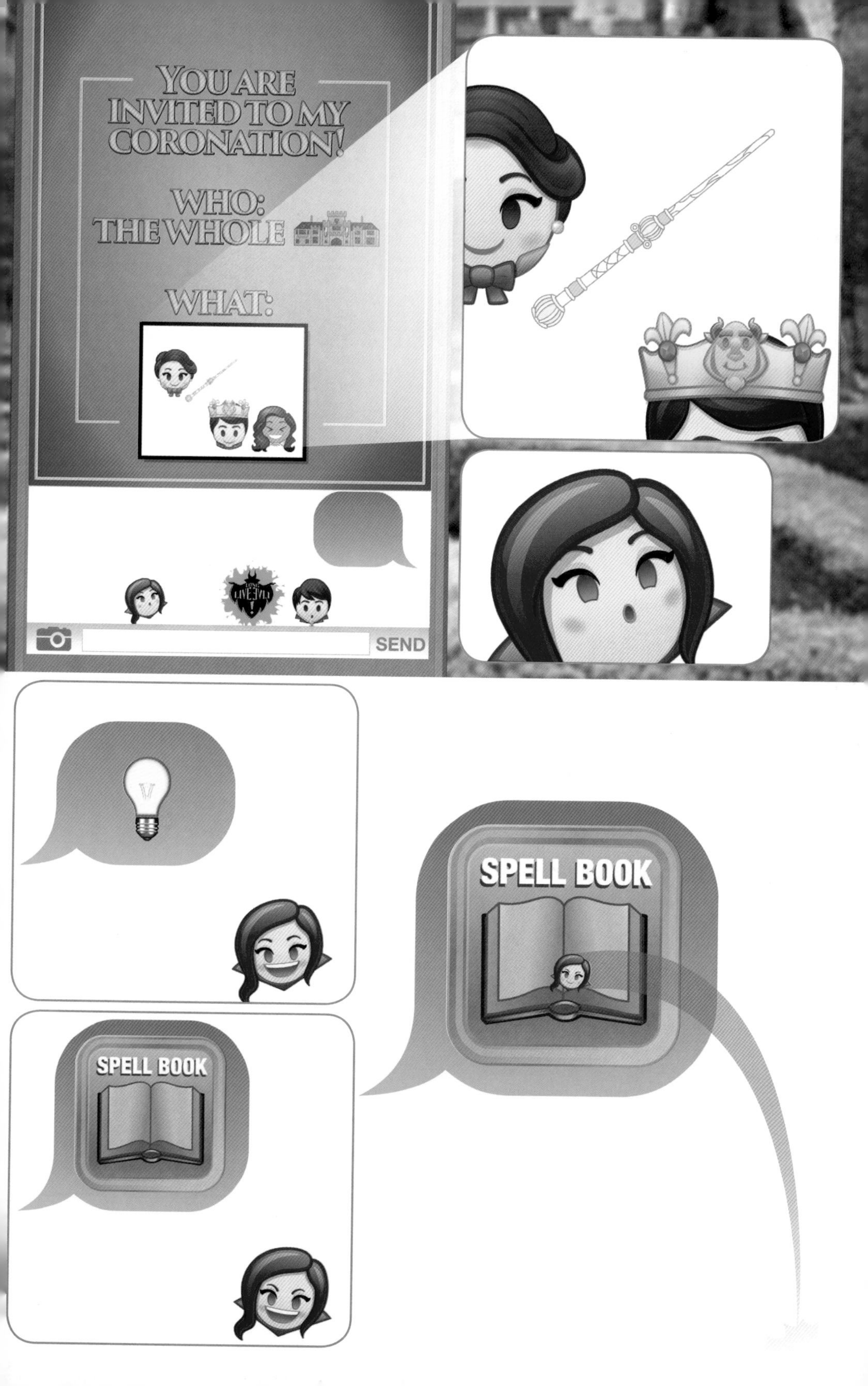
YOU ARE INVITED TO MY CORONATION!
WHO: THE WHOLE
WHAT:
SEND
SPELL BOOK
SPELL BOOK

LOVE POTION RECIPE

serves: 1

ingredients

- [ ]
- [ ]
- [ ]
- [ ]
- [ ]

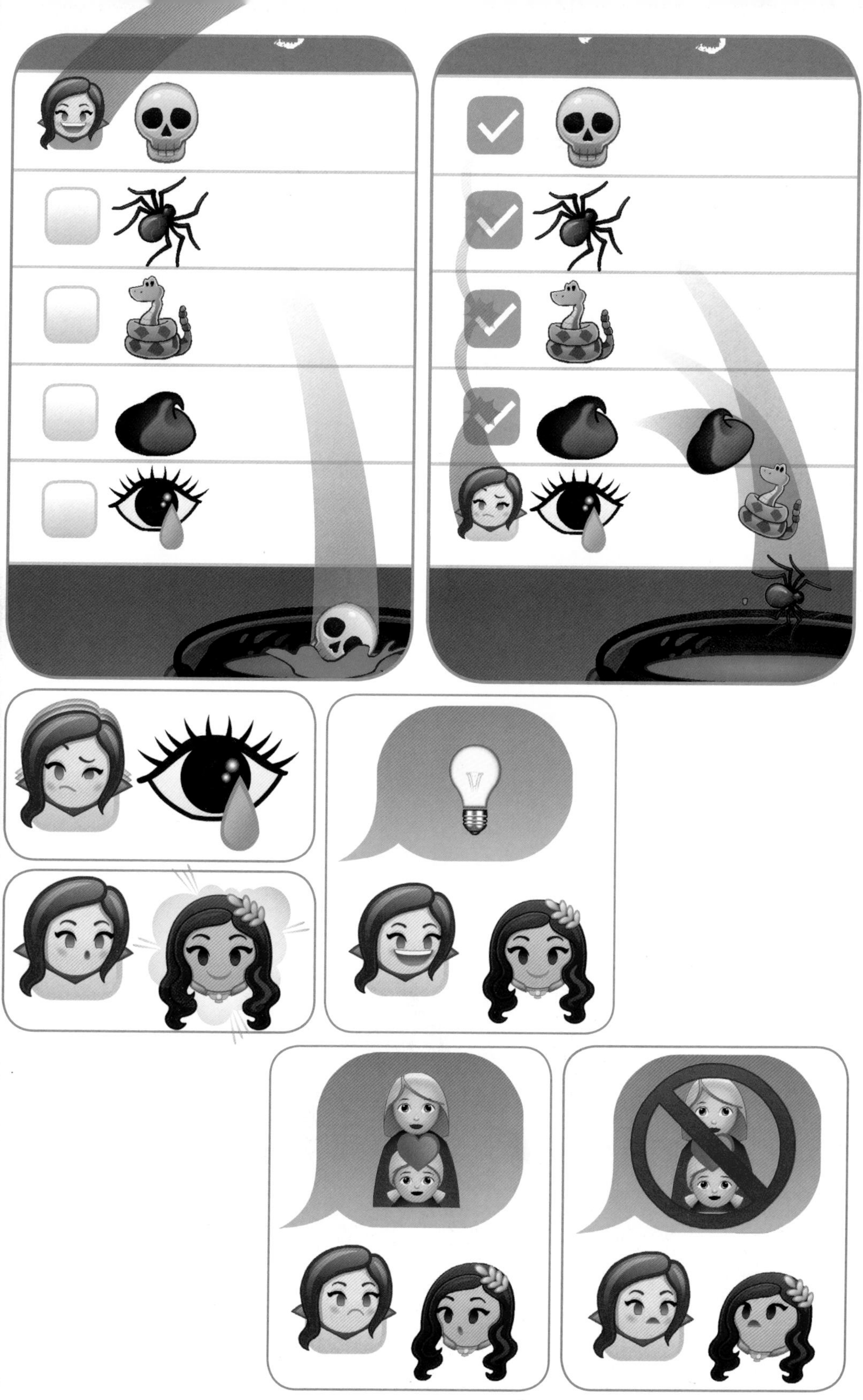

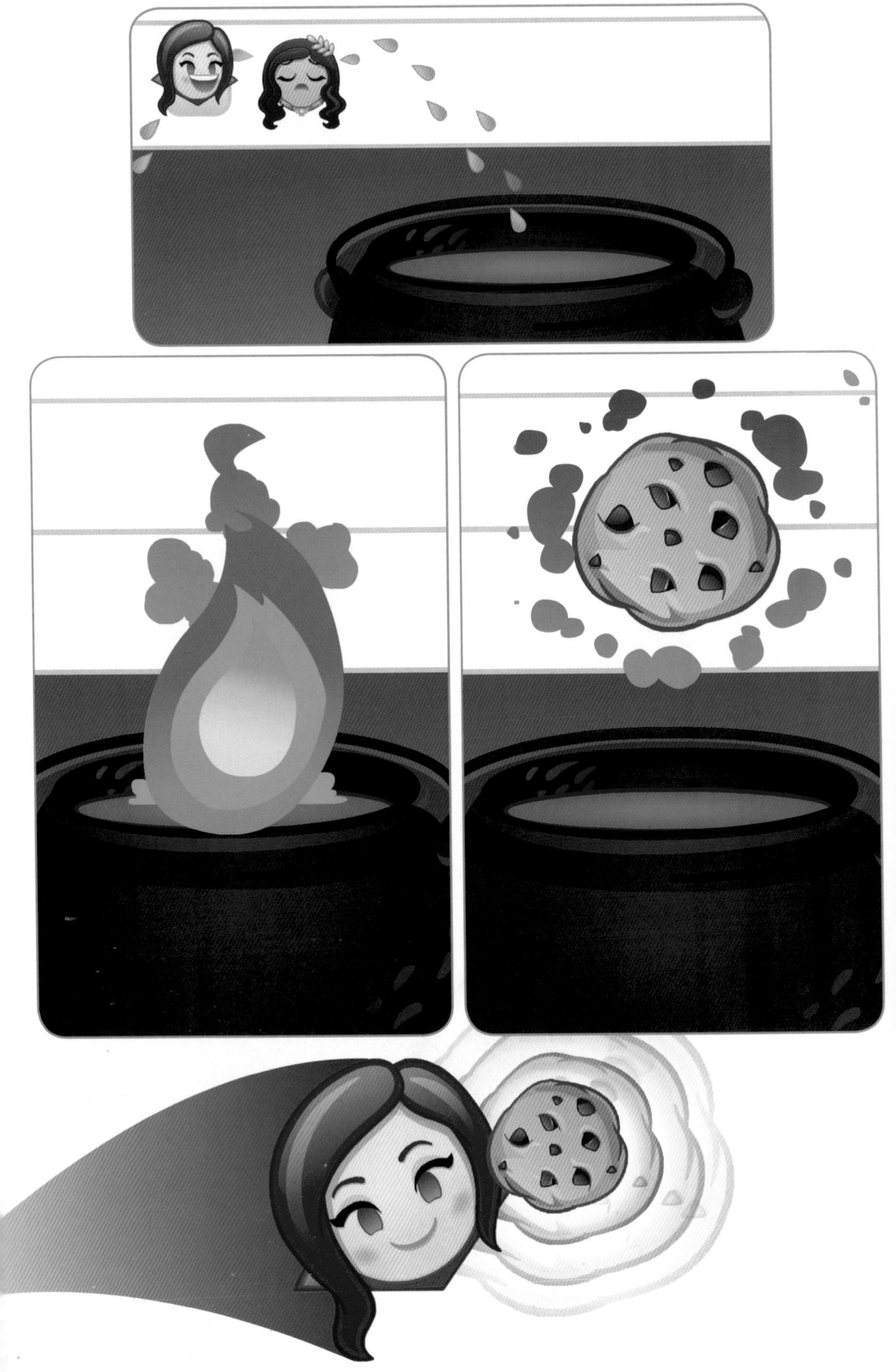

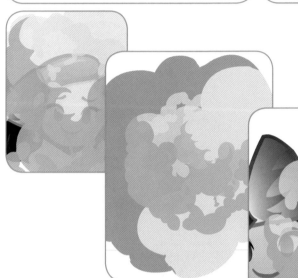

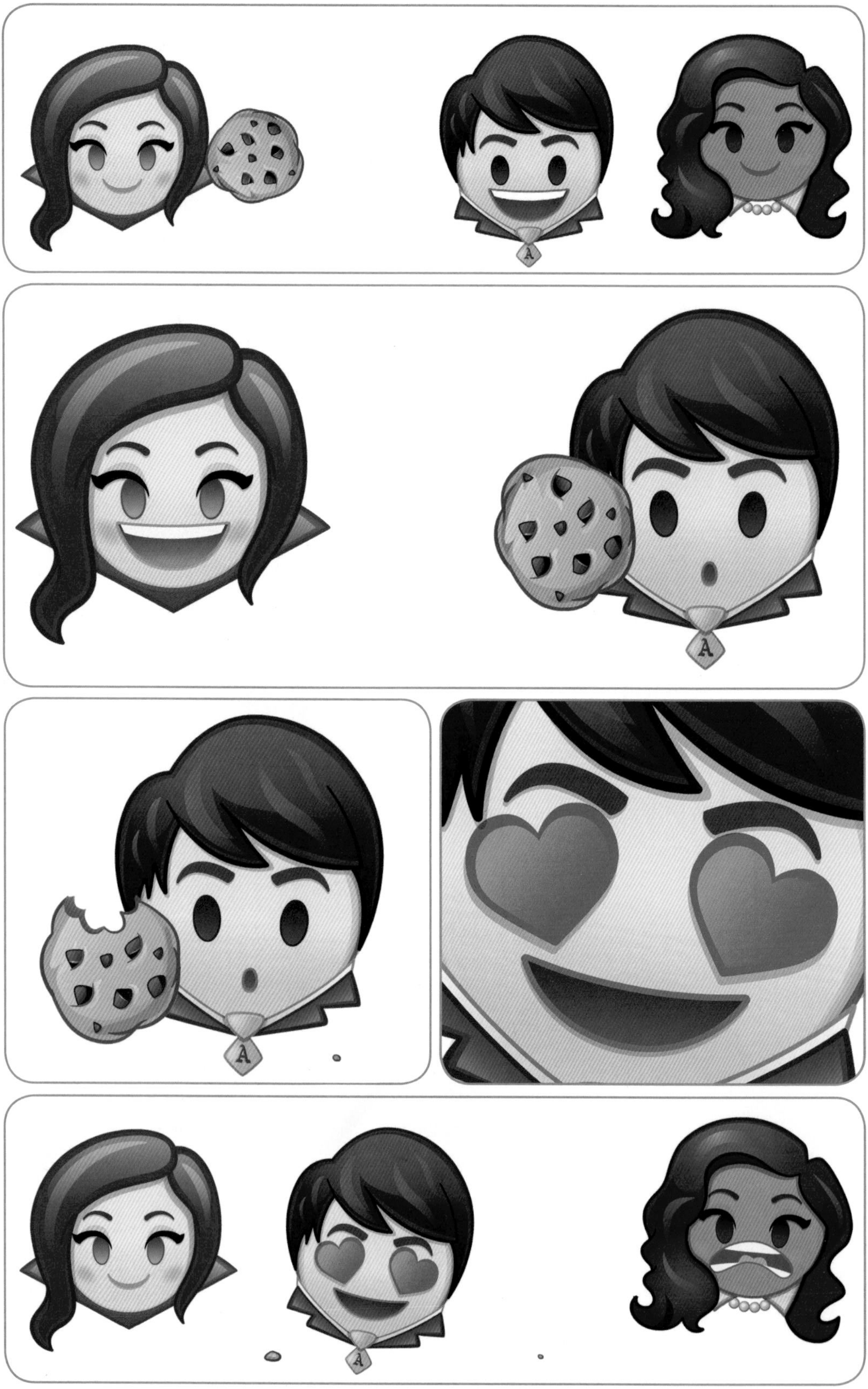

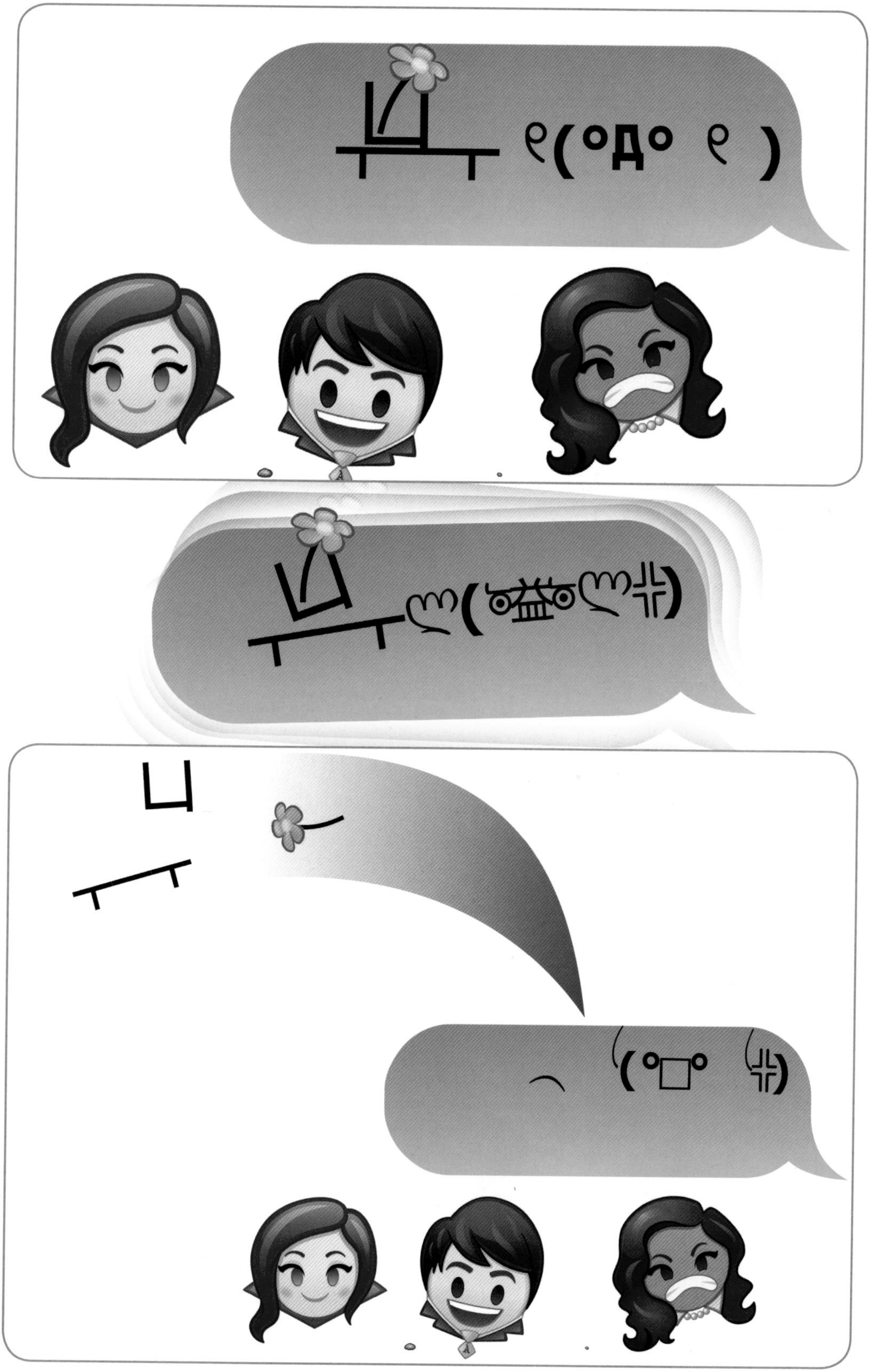
٩(ºдº ٩)
(╬ º□º)╯

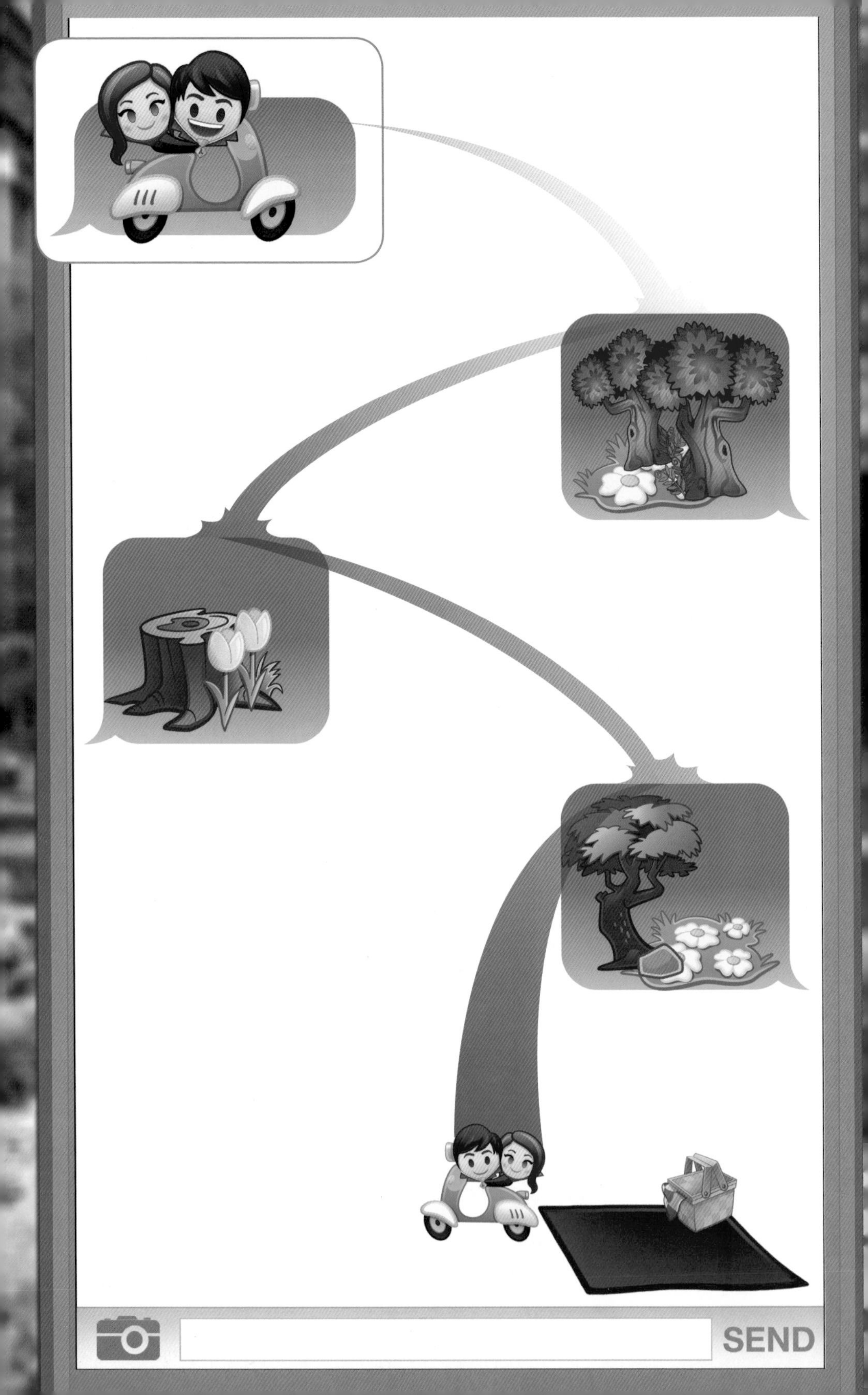
SEND

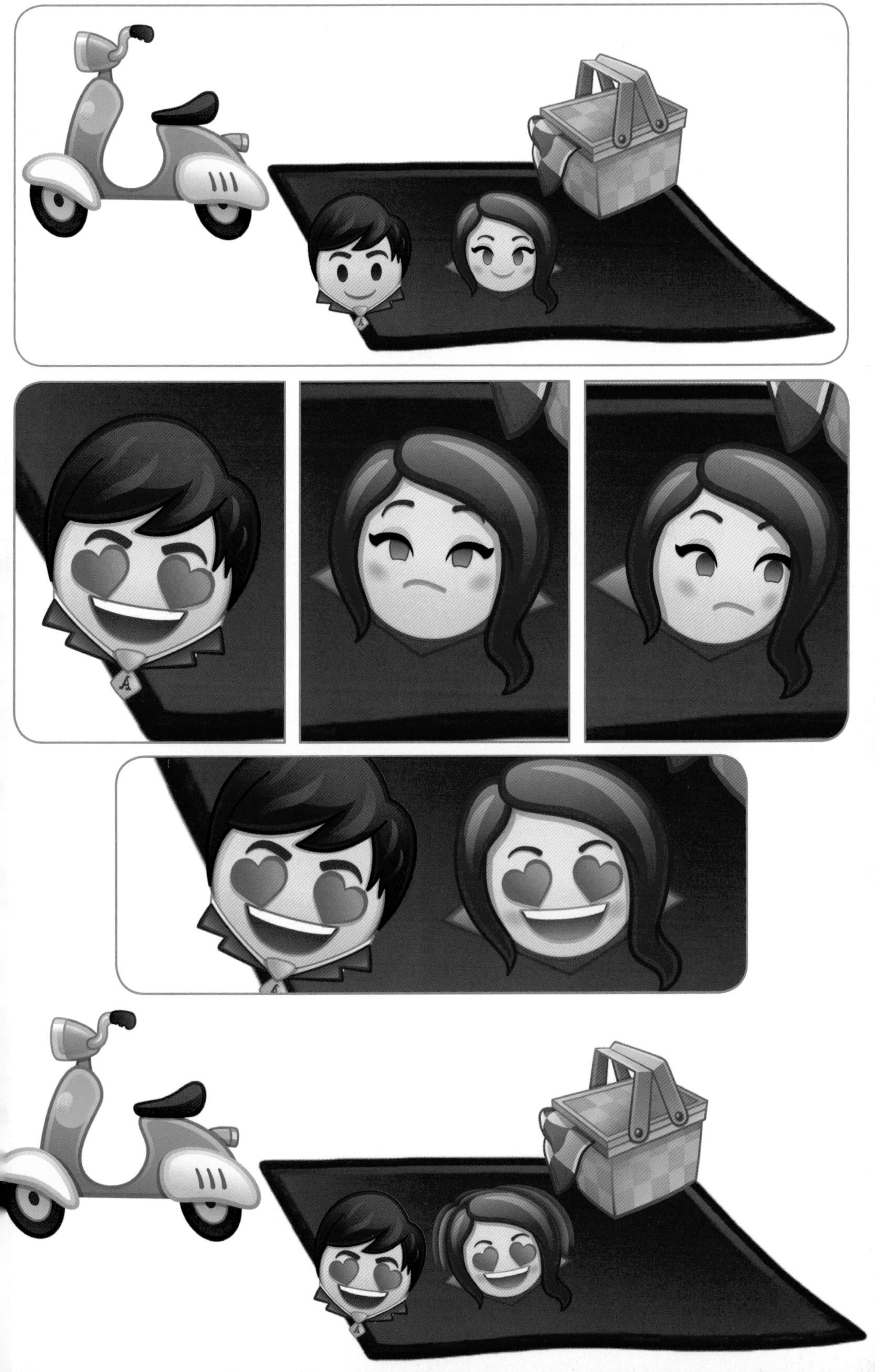

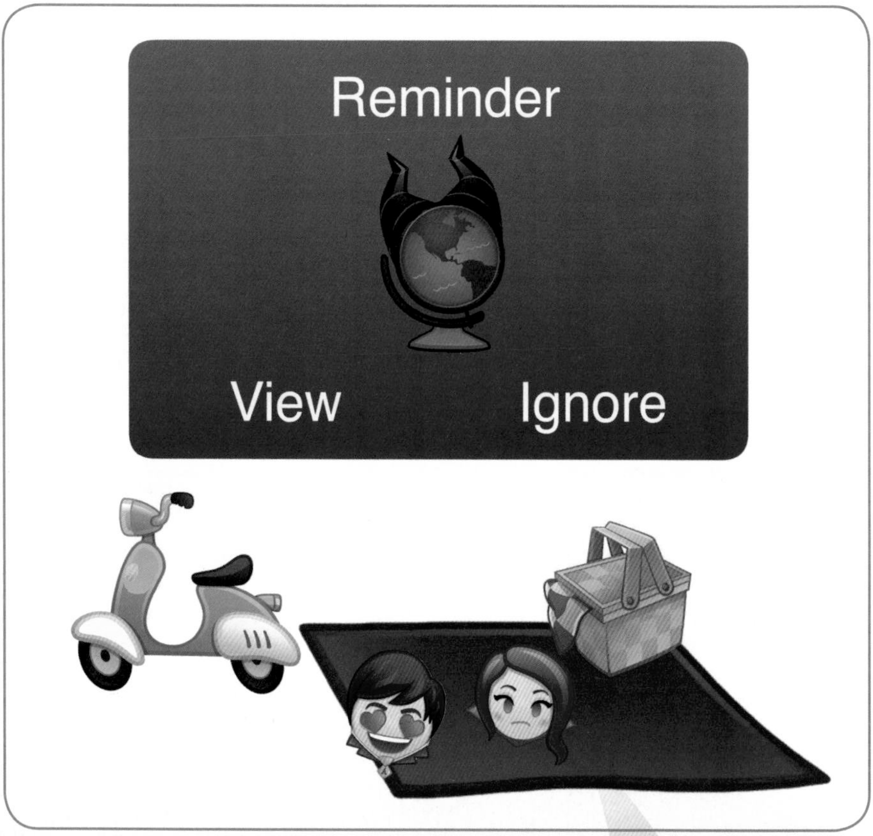
Reminder
View
Ignore

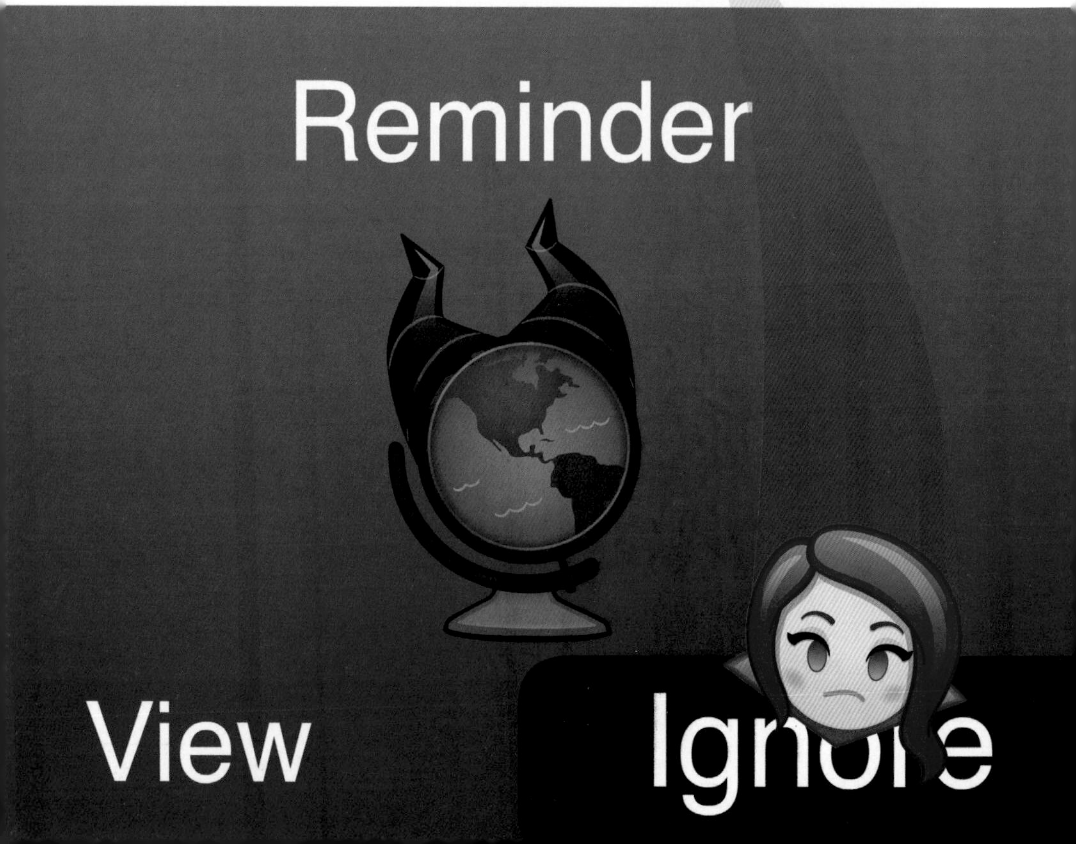
Reminder
View

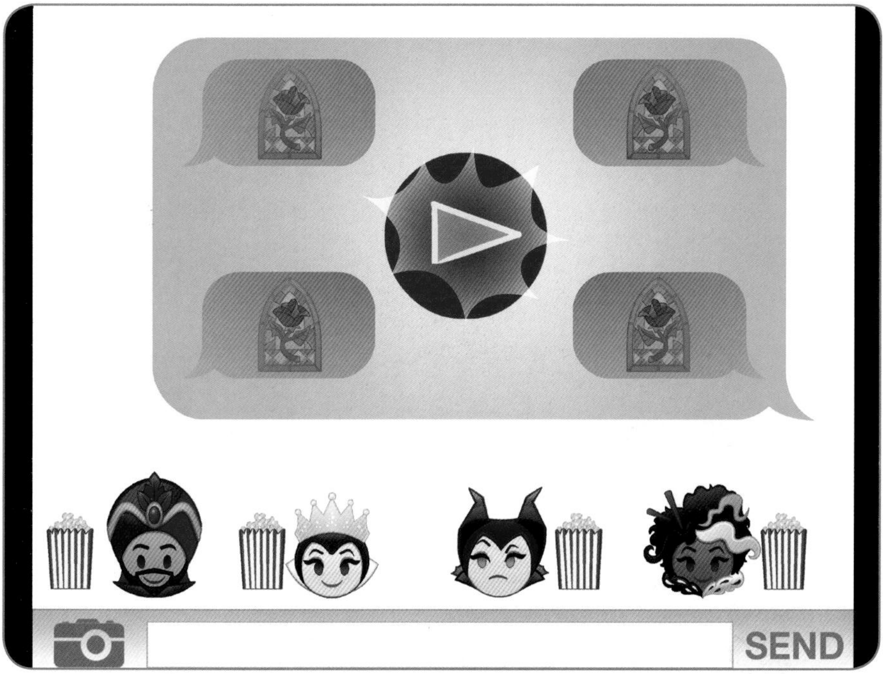
SEND

Coronation day! The villains on the Isle tune in live

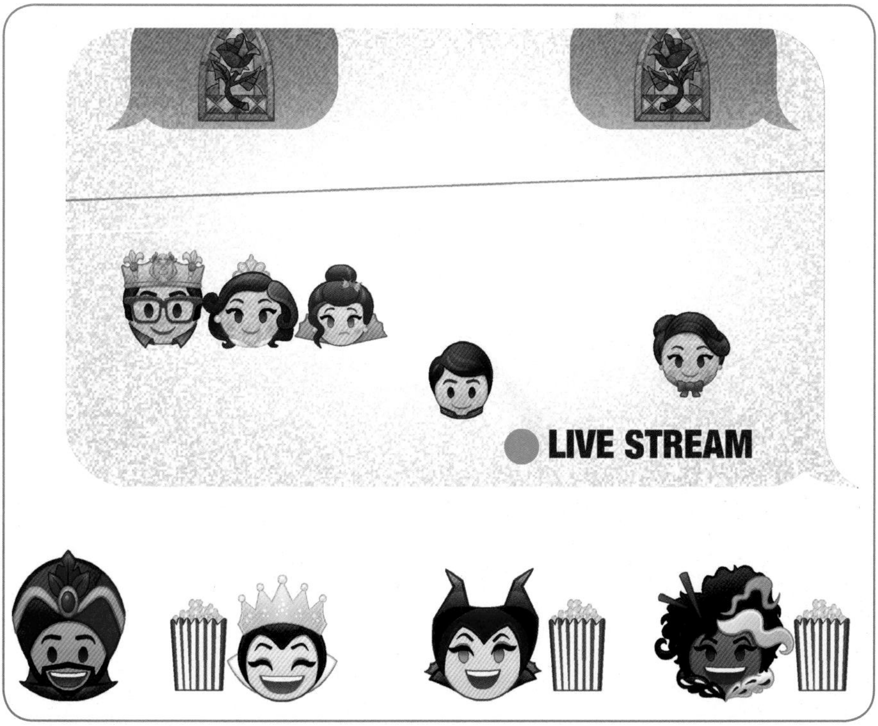
LIVE STREAM

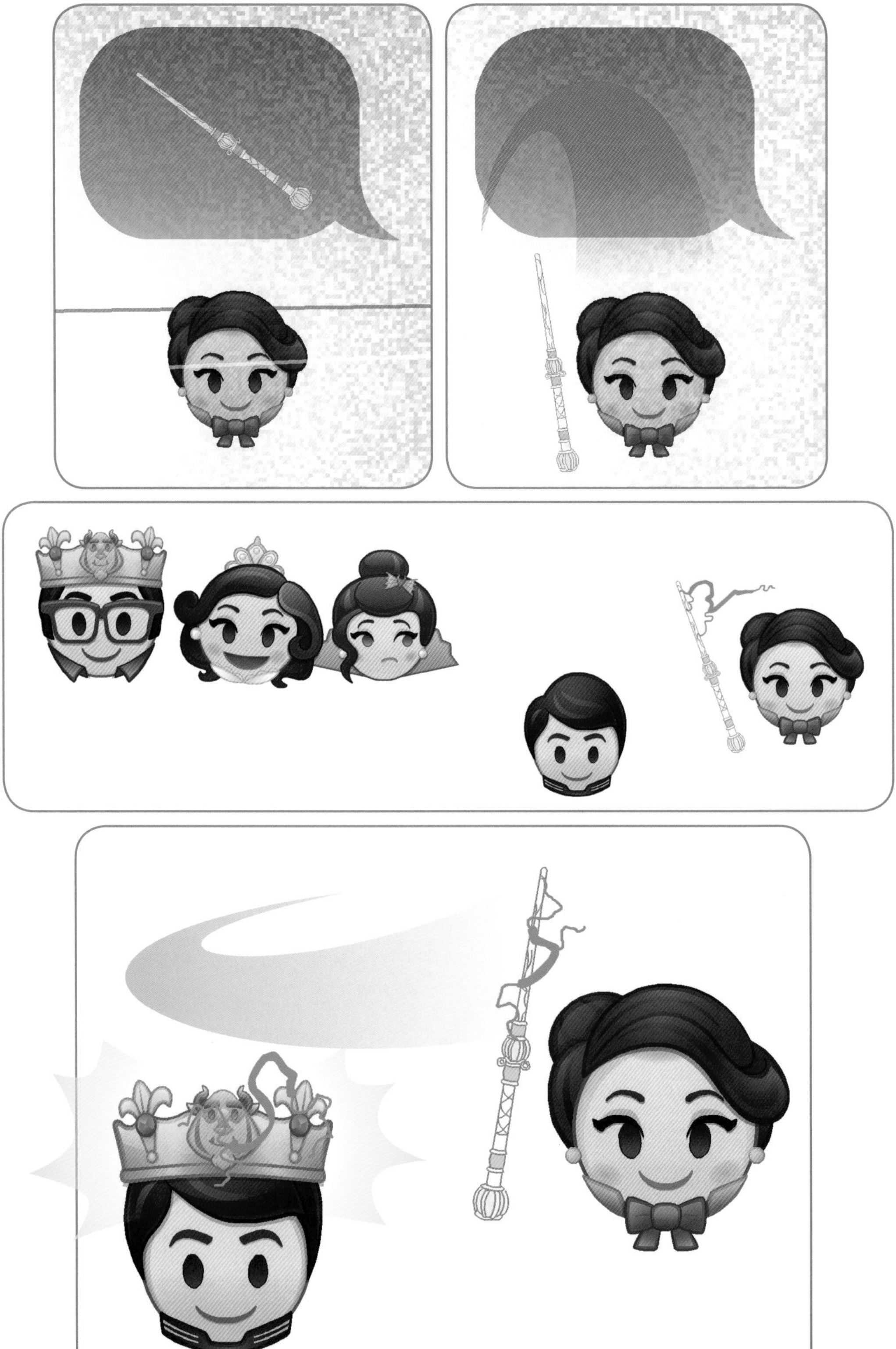

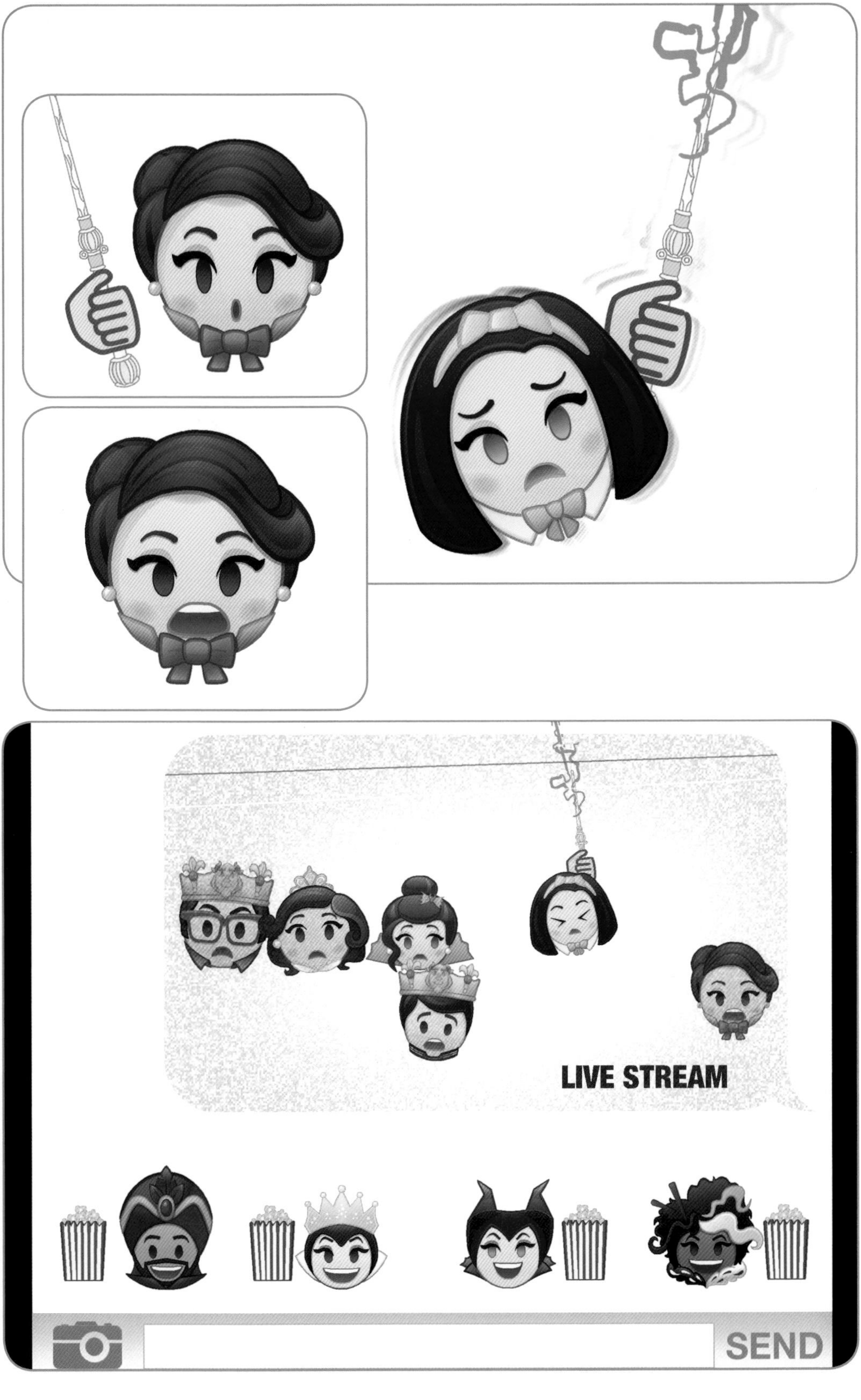
LIVE STREAM
SEND

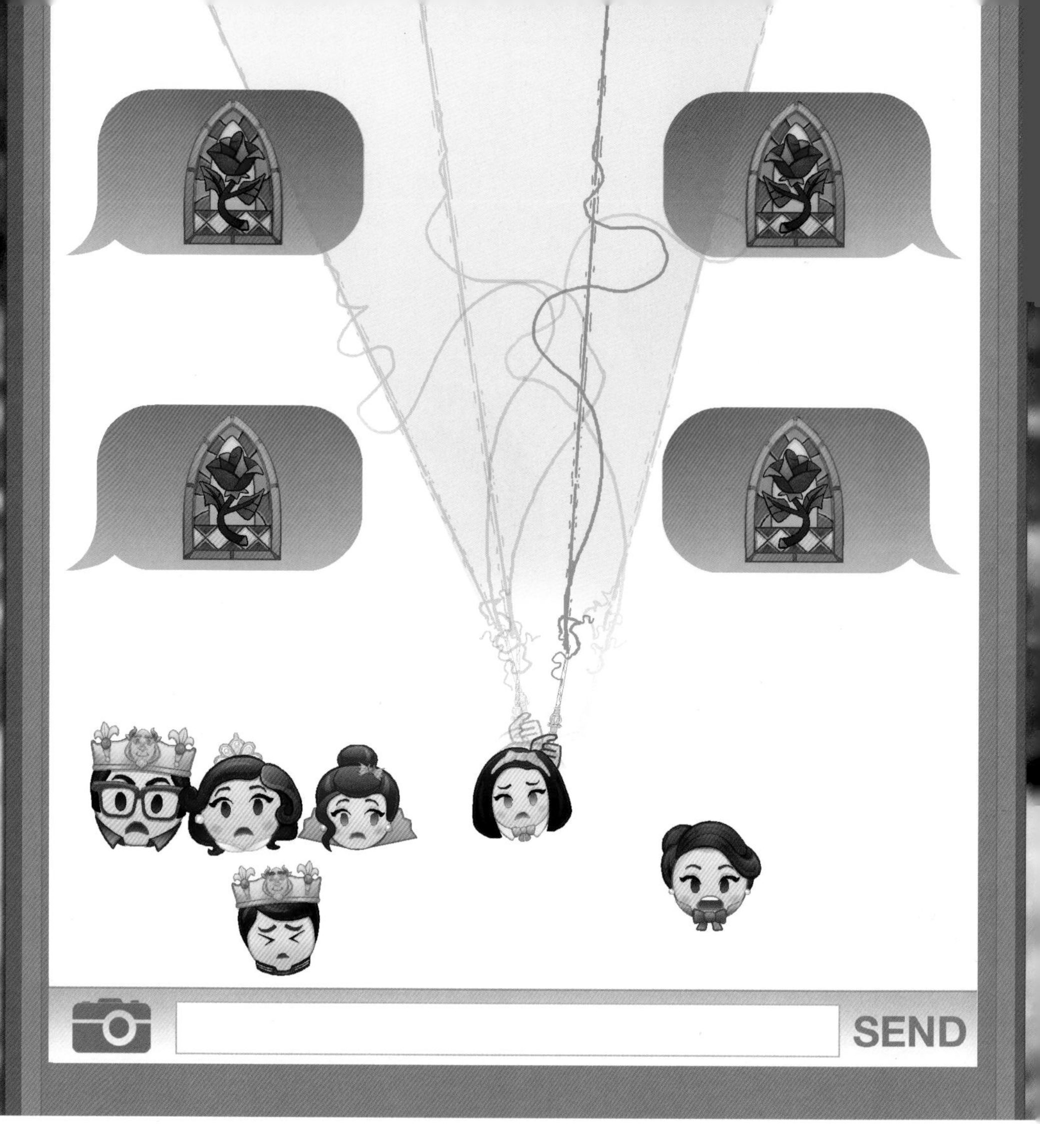
SEND

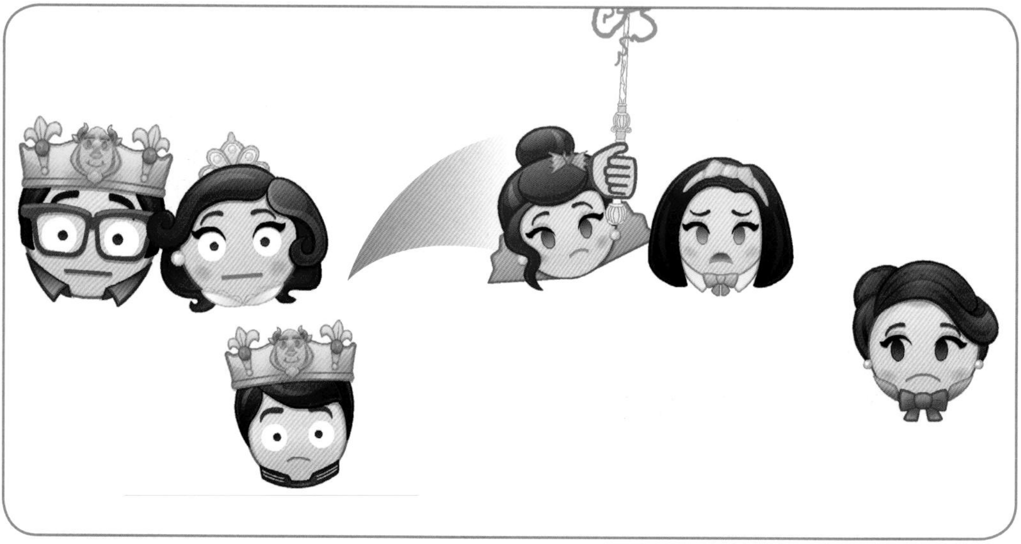

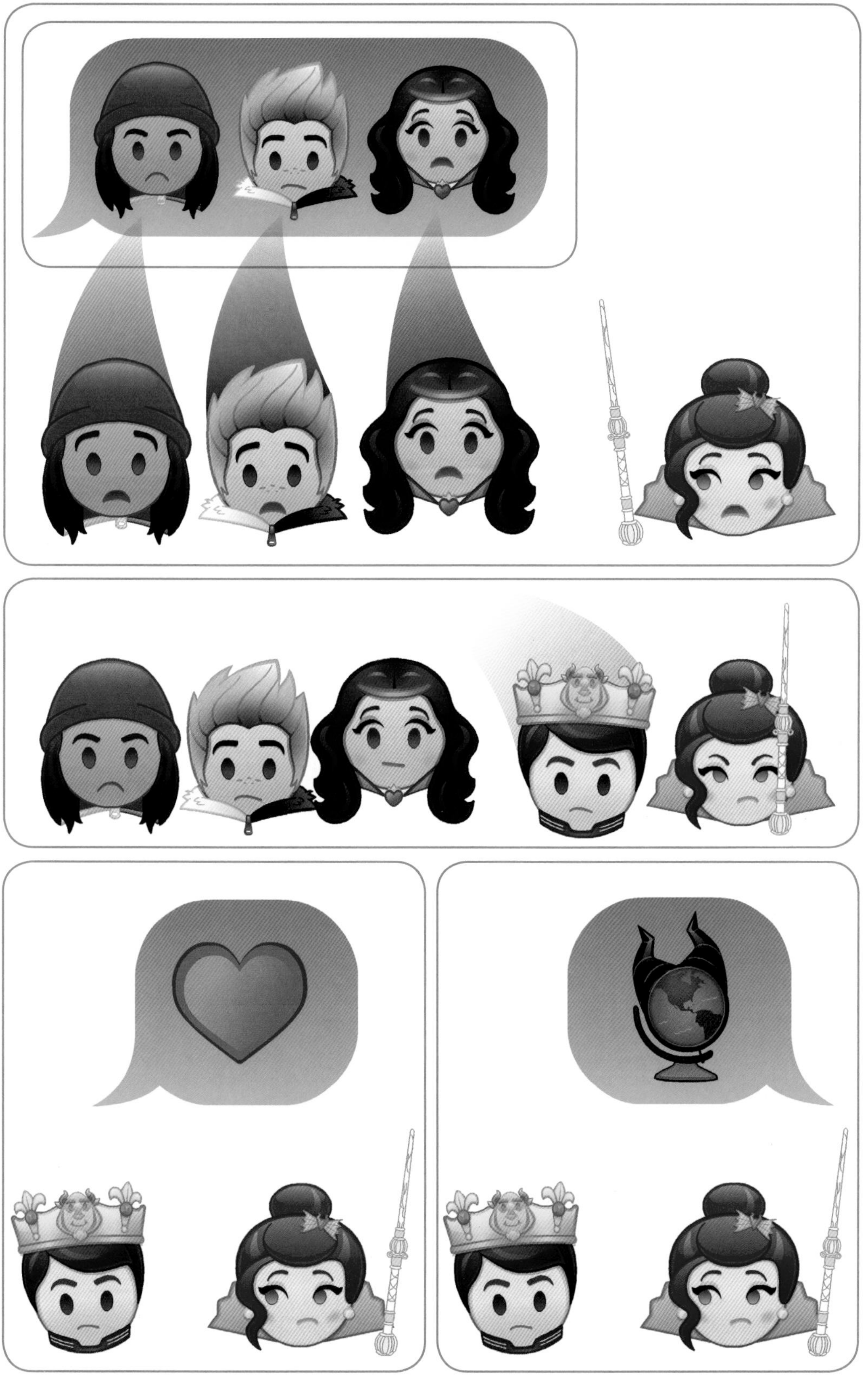

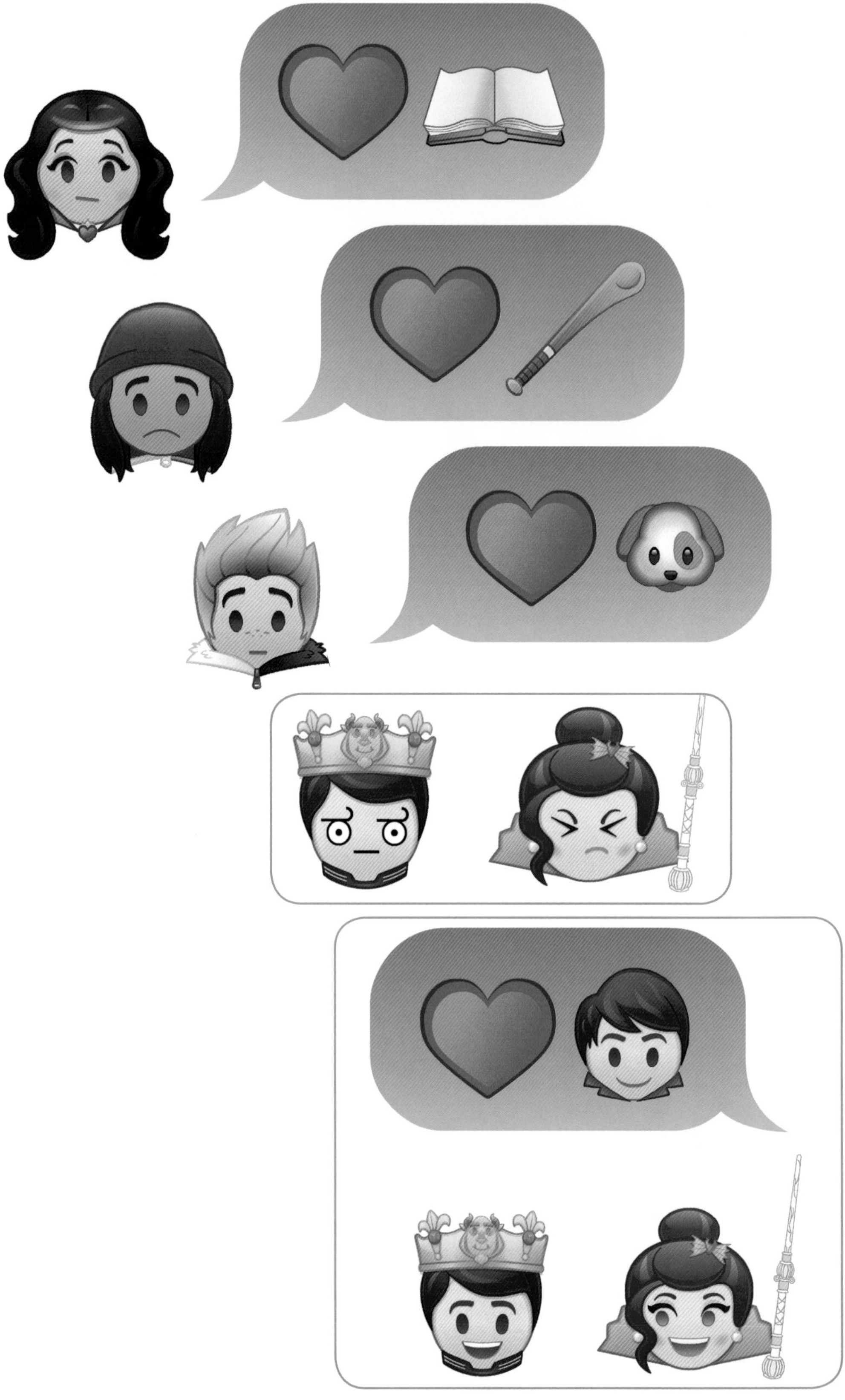

SEND

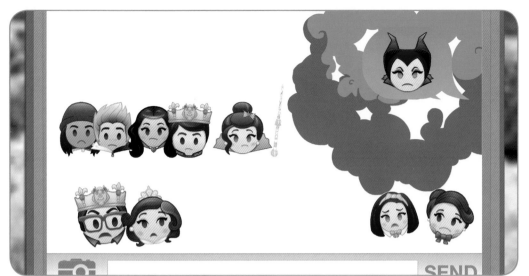

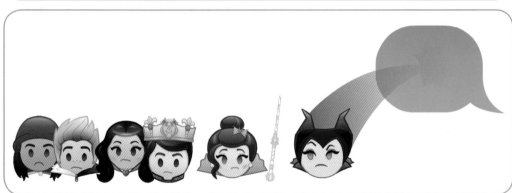

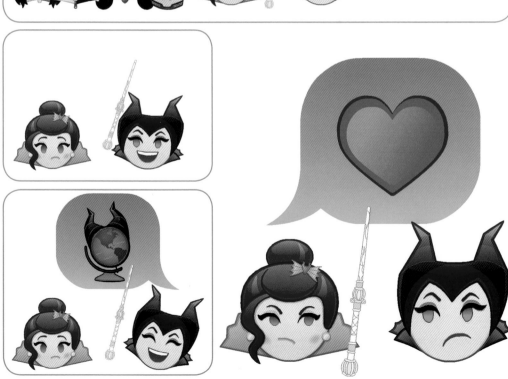

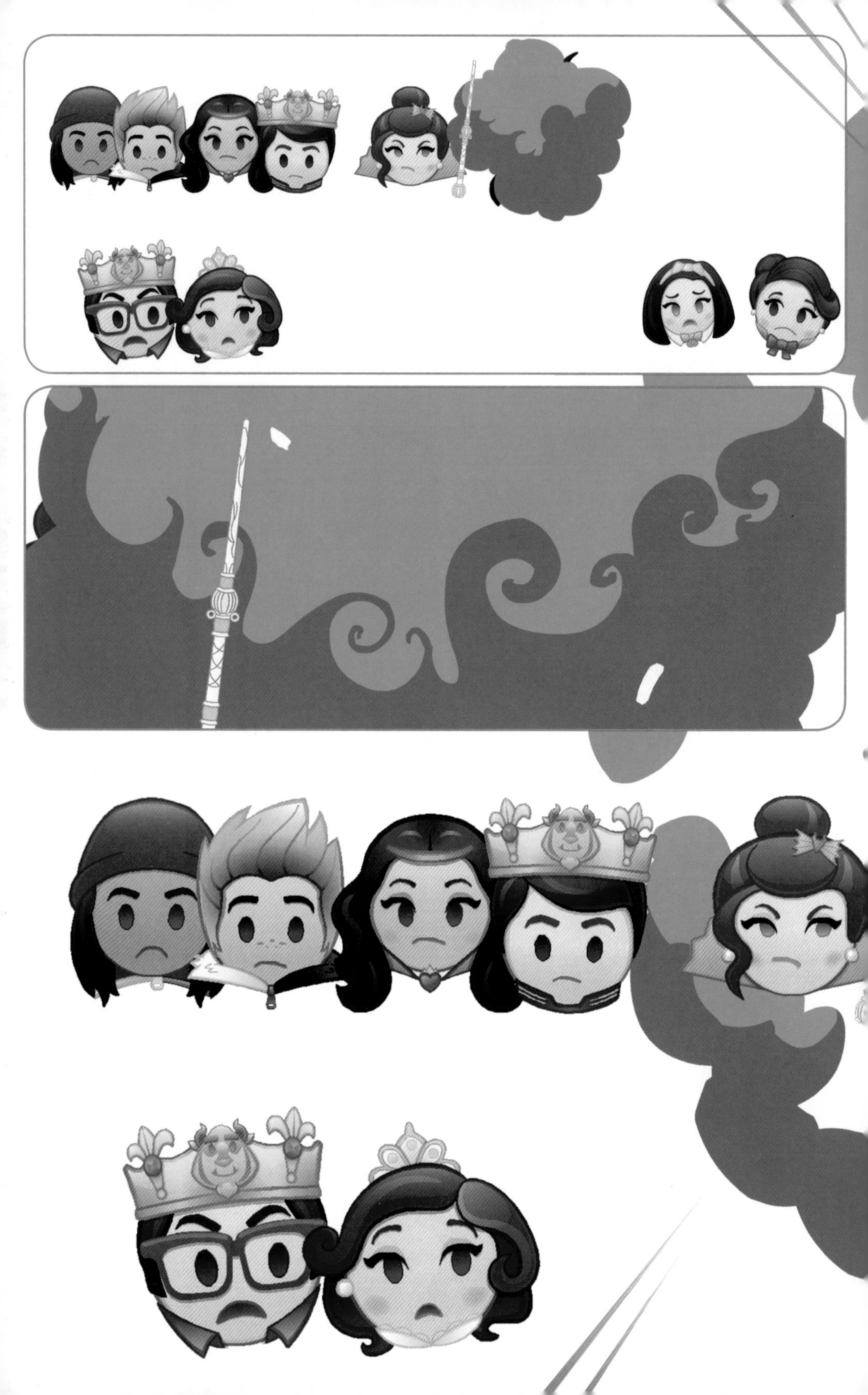

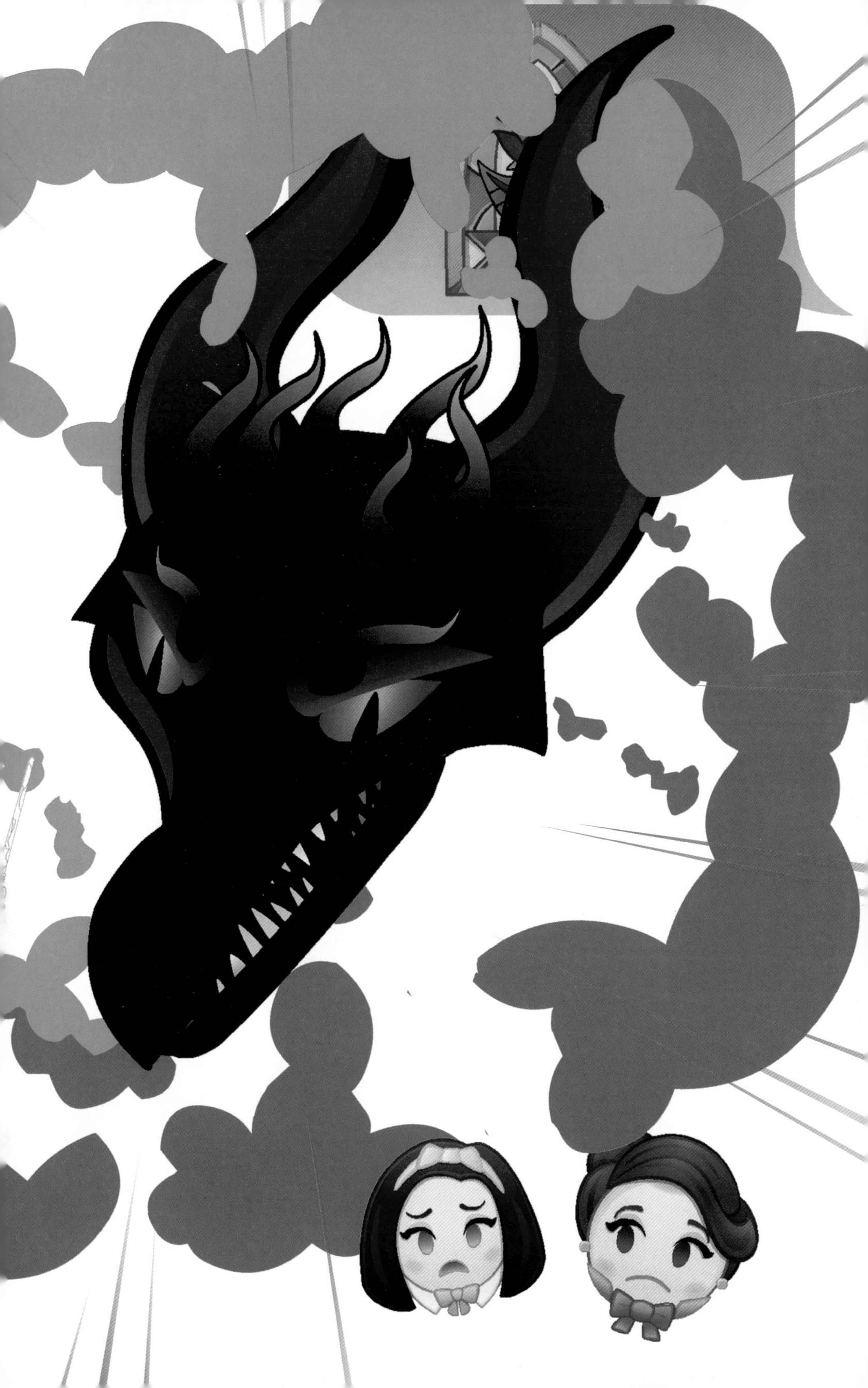

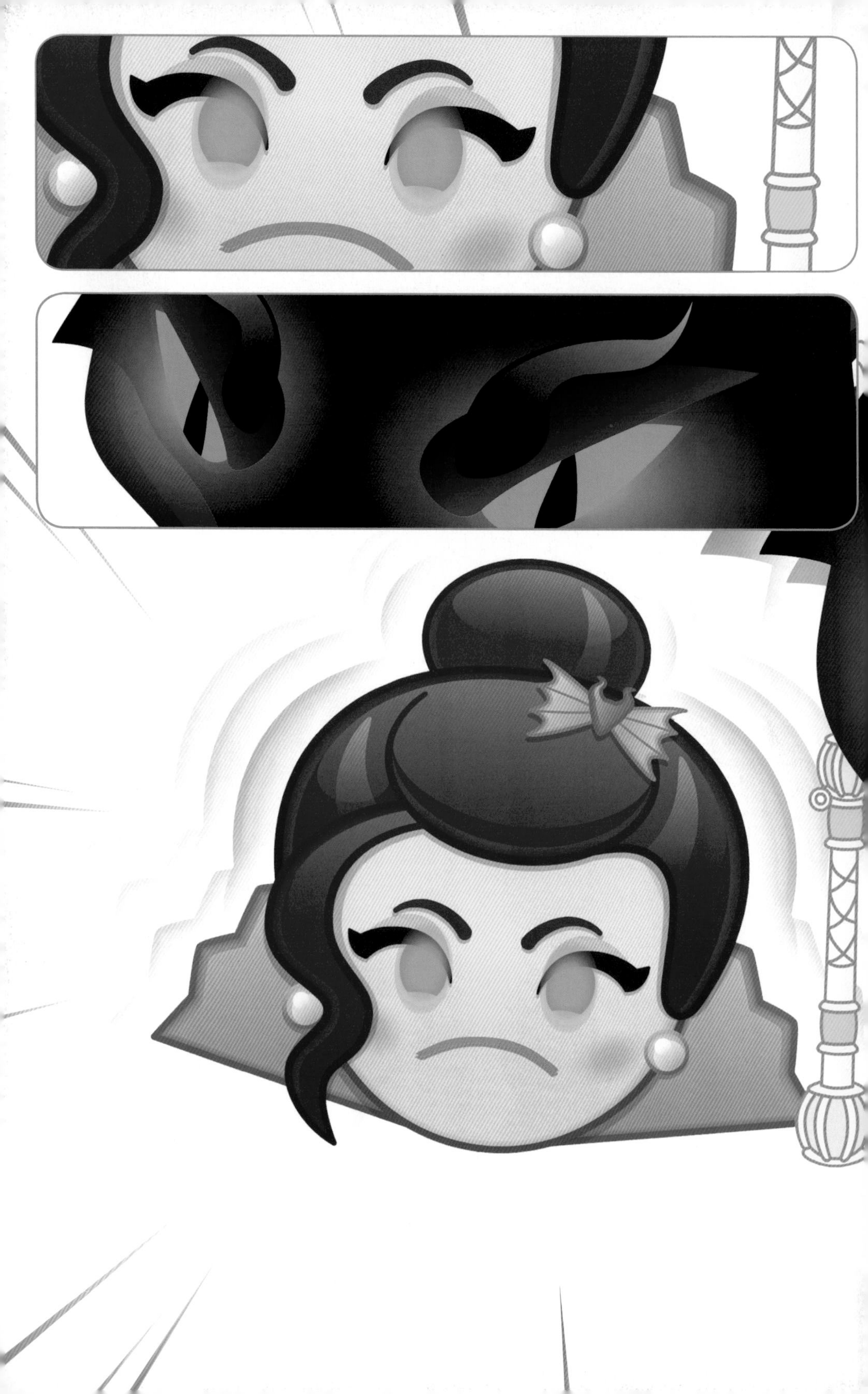

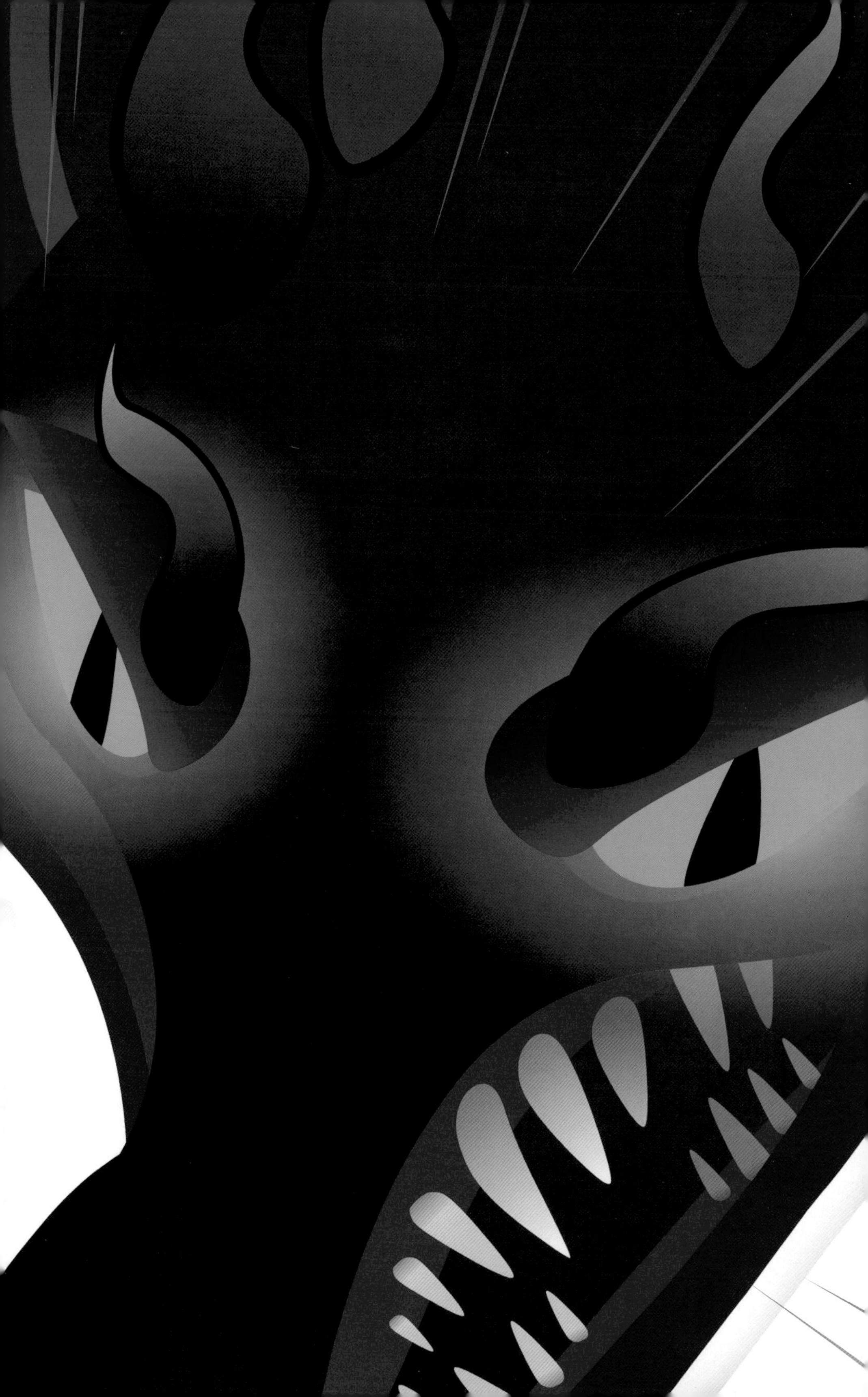

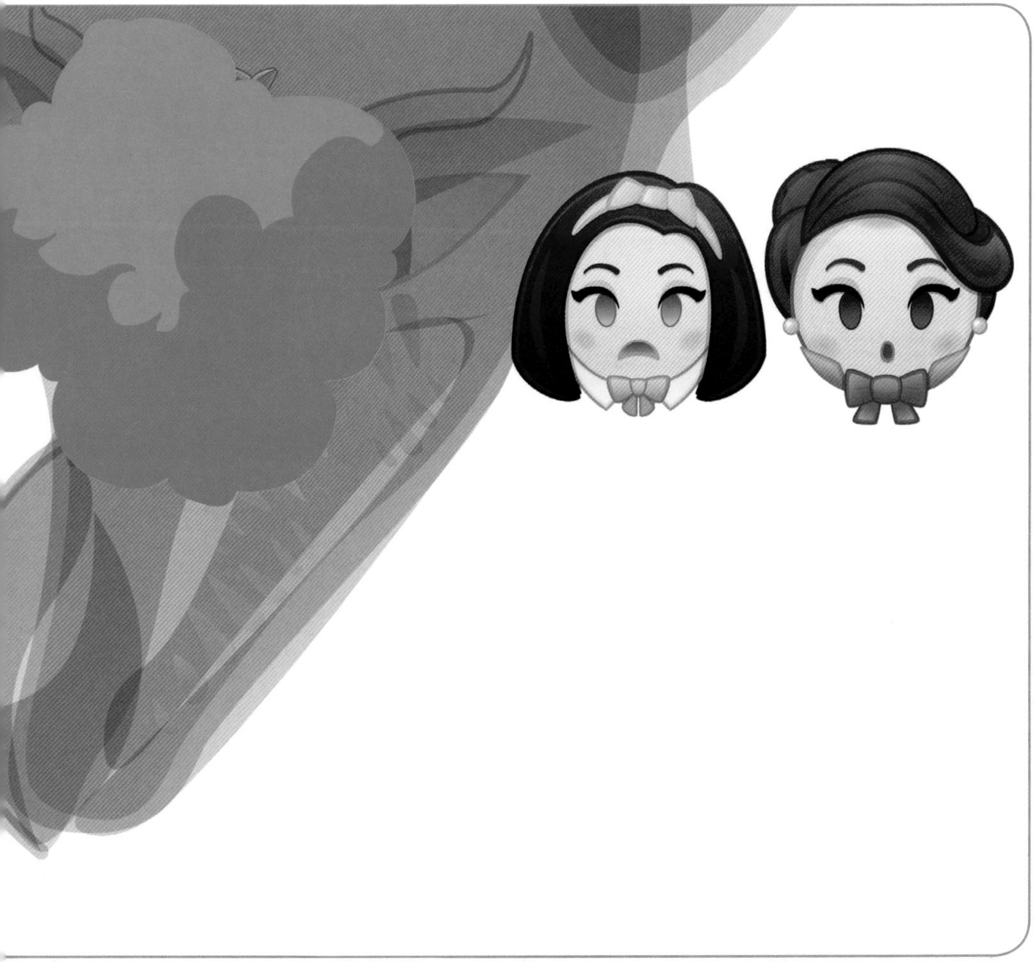

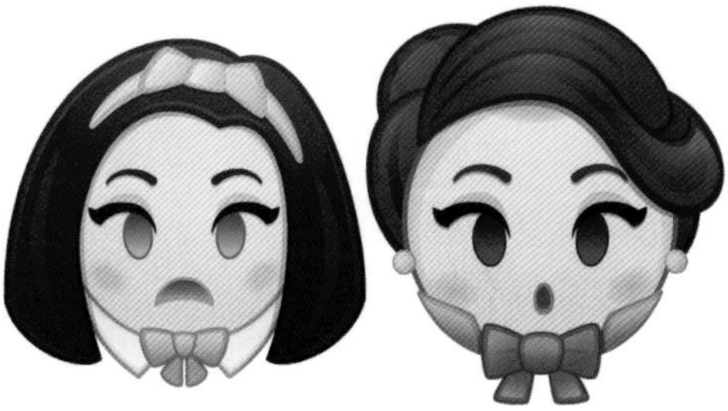

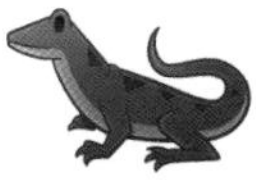

The End

Mal

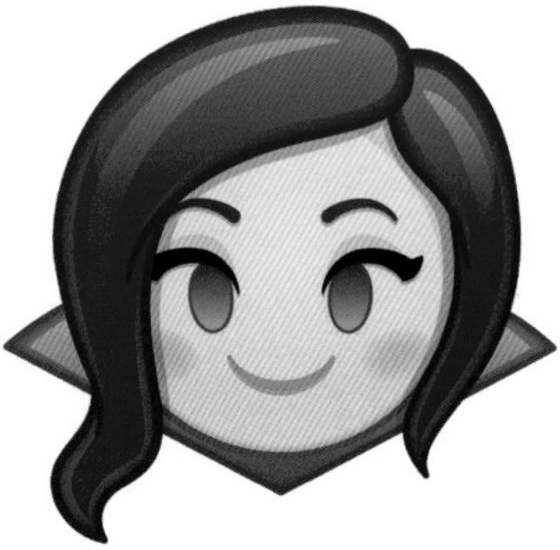

Mal is the daughter of and she's rotten to the . When and her three best friends are invited to , her mom hatches a plan to free all the villains from the Isle once and for all. Will help her mom make Auradon ? Or will her new friendship with make good the new bad?

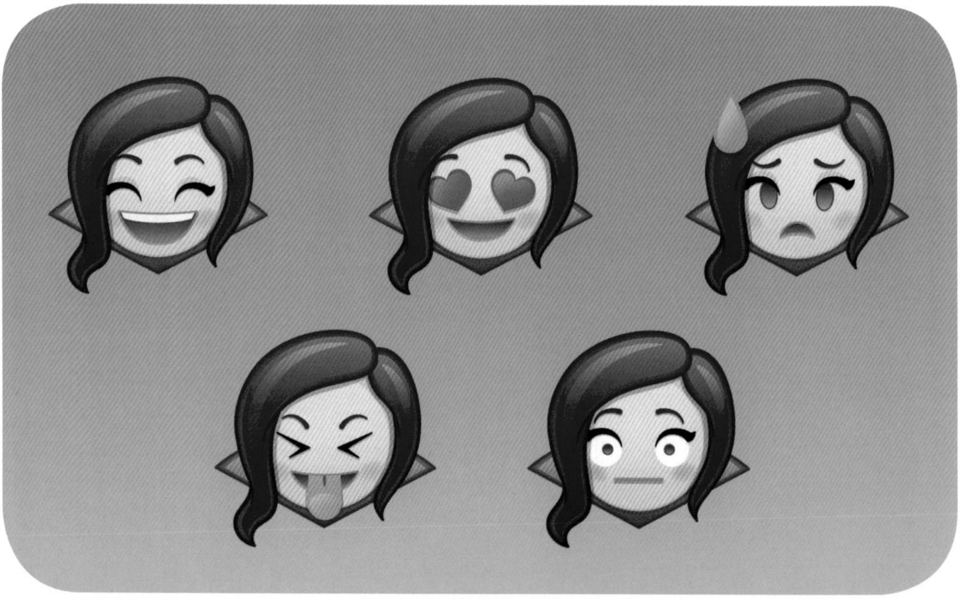

Evie

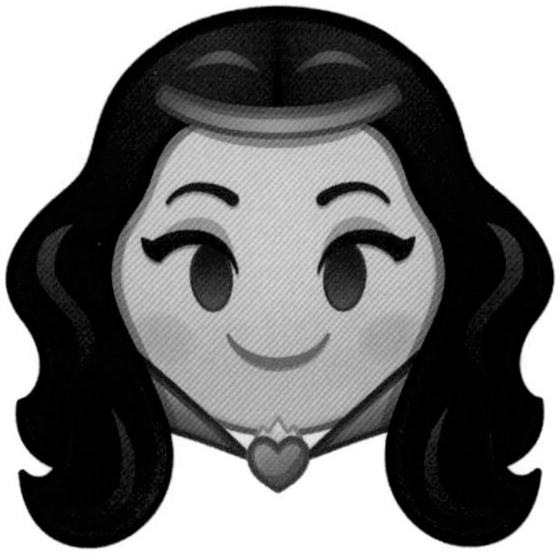

Unlike the other VKs, Evie, daughter of , is excited to go to 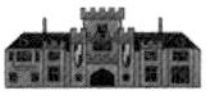 and maybe meet her . More than just the fairest of them all, 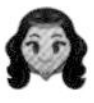 has serious  skills that she uses to help 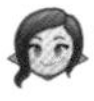 with her plan to steal the .

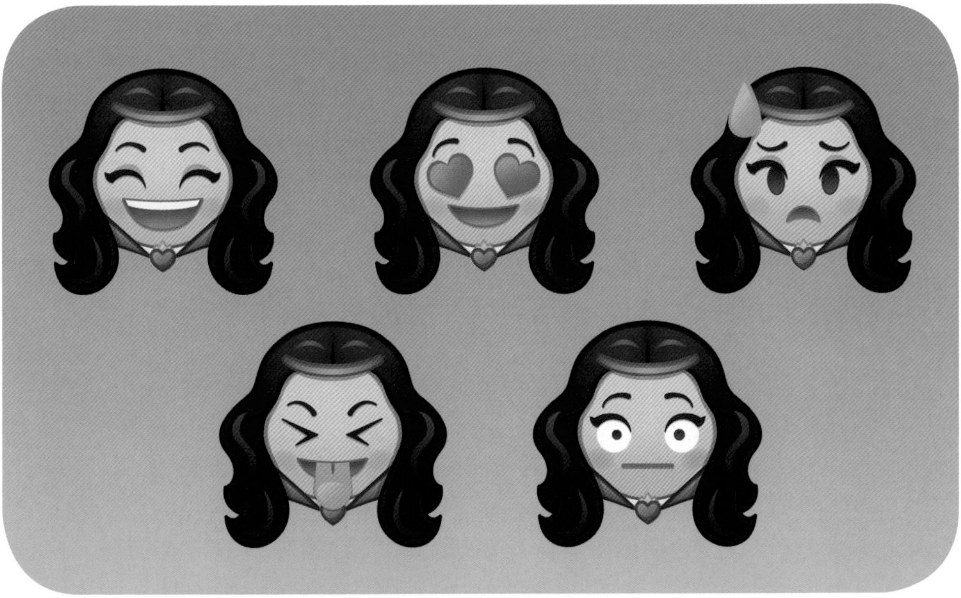

Carlos

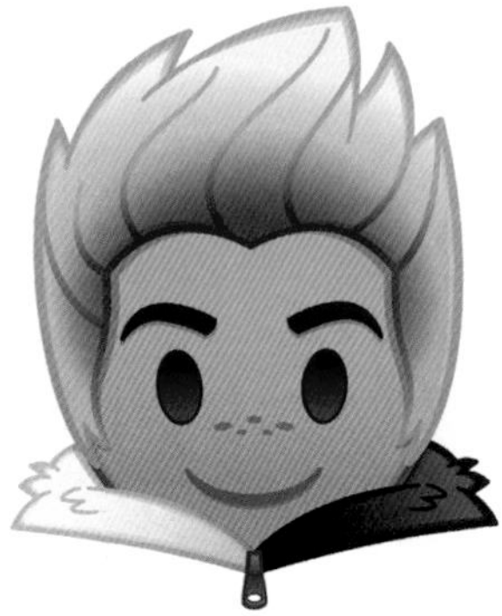

Despite being the son of [emoji], Carlos is firmly [emoji]. As [emoji] and the other VKs work to free their parents from the Isle, [emoji]'s tech skills help them out along the way.

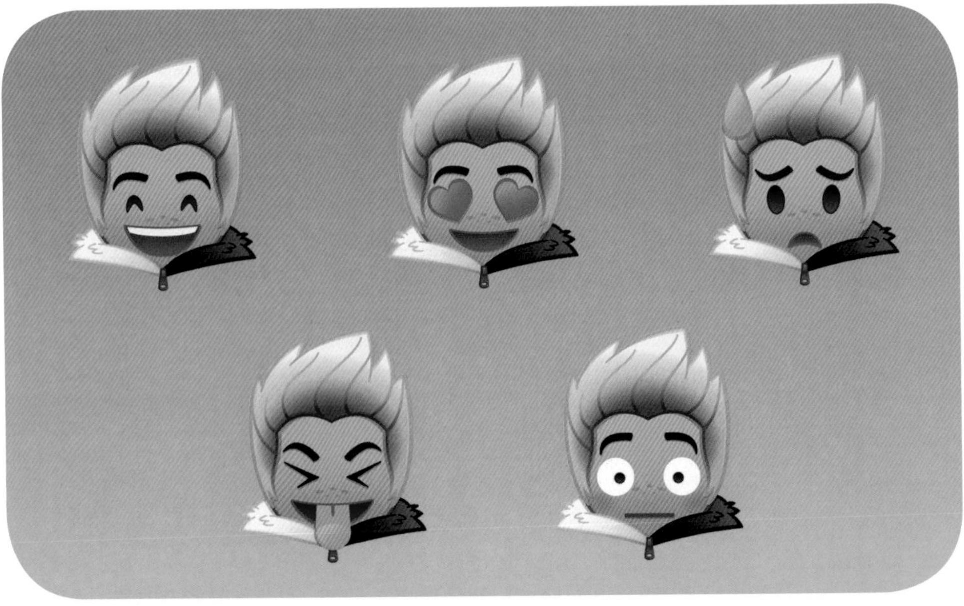

Jay

The son of 👺, Jay is a handsome and athletic thief from the Isle who helps 👹 with her plan to steal the ⚕. Together with 👩, 👩, and 👦, 👩 is one of the first VKs to go to 🏰.

Collect them all!

As Told By
Disney emoji

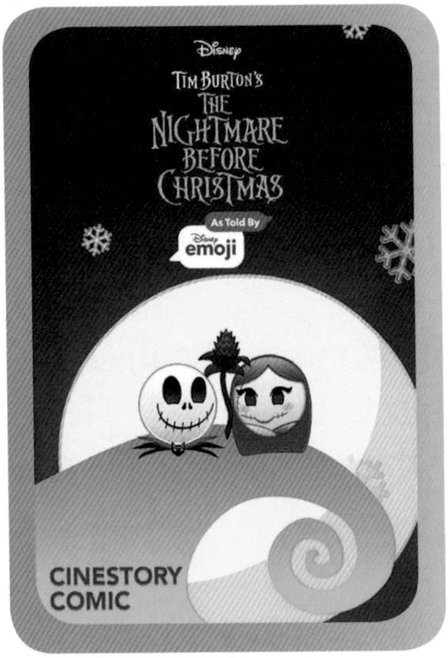
Disney
Tim Burton's
The
Nightmare
Before
Christmas
As Told By
Disney emoji
CINESTORY
COMIC
Tim Burton's The Nightmare Before Christmas As Told By Emoji

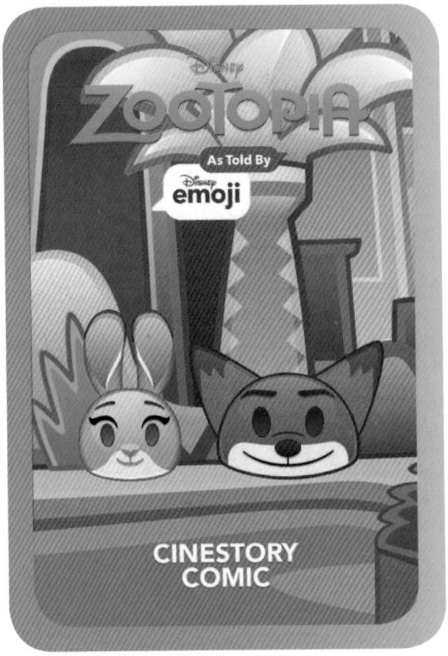
Disney
Zootopia
As Told By
Disney emoji
CINESTORY
COMIC
Zootopia As Told By Emoji

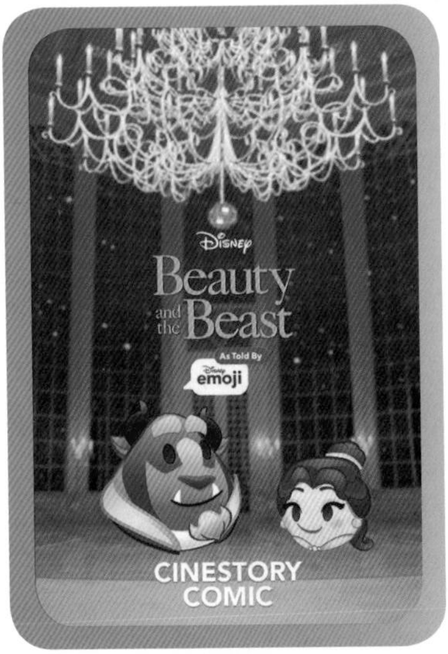
Disney
Beauty and the Beast
As Told By
Disney emoji
CINESTORY
COMIC
Beauty and the Beast As Told By Emoji

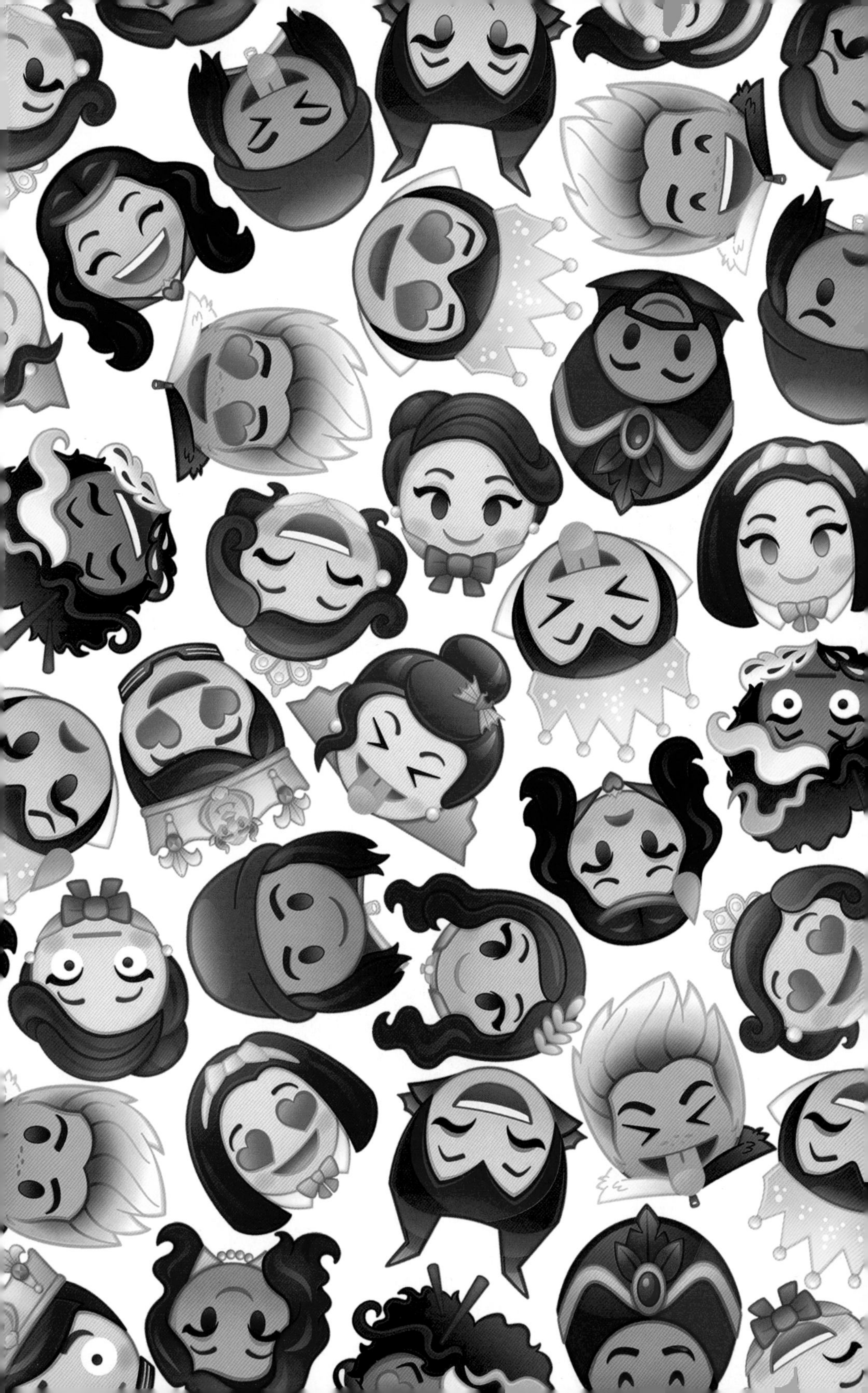

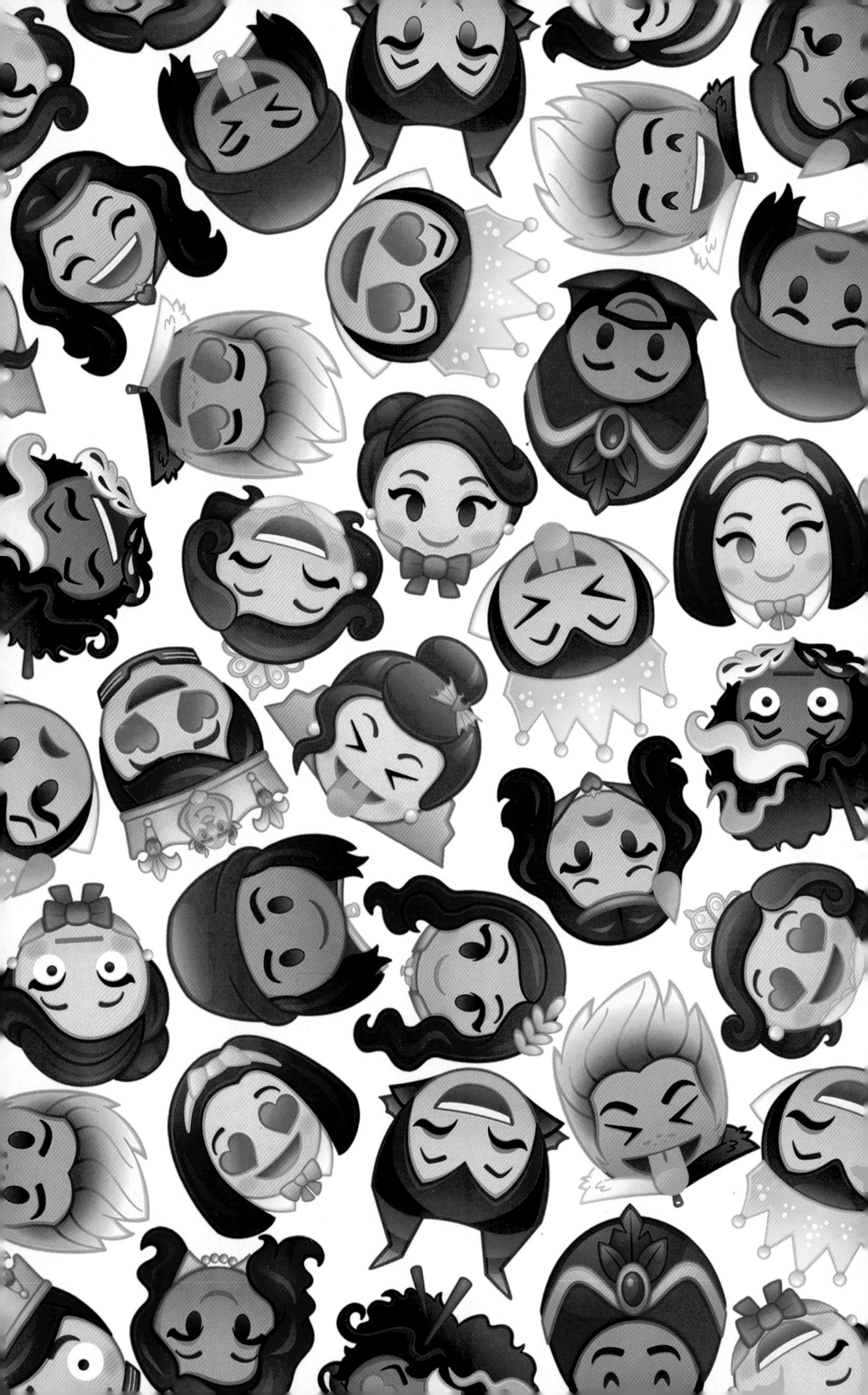